The Lady In The Movies

The Lady In The Movies

RONALD HIGGINS

ARPress
45 Dan Road Suite 5
Canton MA 02021
Hotline: 1(888) 821-0229
Fax: 1(508) 545-7580

Ordering Information:
Quantity sales. Special discounts are available on quantity purchases by corporations, associations, and others. For details, contact the publisher at the address above.

Printed in the United States of America.

ISBN-13:   Softcover   979-8-89330-478-7
                    eBook   979-8-89330-479-4

Library of Congress Control Number: 2024901224

DEDICATION

I am dedicating this book to my two friends Jack Terrano and Lorrie, his wife from California. It was their support that made this book possible.

Contents

ONE

My name is Sam Ryan, and I'm a P.I., and I'm back in Los Angeles,where it all started. Sometimes I get the impression I'm not very good at what I do, but then when the job is complete, I realize I did a pretty good job. However, this last case left a bad taste in my mouth; it had been six months since I left Kathy and her father and the memory of Aunt Gladys.

Kathy was a promising police person with the Burbank Police Force. Then she met me. I came out here for the reading of my uncle's will and ended up going to a funeral. Aunt Gladys only wanted to help, and now she is dead. I blame myself for her death because I should not have gotten her involved. I don't think I will ever forget her. Kathy had recovered from her wounds and surgery, something she shouldn't have had to go through at all.

That, too, was my fault. The case is solved and closed, and I must get on with it.

I received a letter while I was in New York closing shop and packing to move back out here for good. It was the lawyer in charge of my aunt's will that contacted me. She left me everything, which was considerable.

That also included the house in Glendale. This is not the way I would have wanted it to turn out, but that's life in the big city, or at least that is the way the saying goes. Sometimes we don't have choices; it just turns out that way. I refused to live at my aunt's house; it would bring back too many memories. I called the lawyer and had him sell the house and put the money in my account. I will have to look for another place to live when I'm ready. I have an idea where I want to live, kind of a combination of office and house. That way, I can work from home. For the time being, Kathy's father said he had an extra room, and I could stay with him.

Kathy's father is a retired policeman for the Burbank police where Kathy was working before, she got involved in my last case and got shot. I can hardly understand him when he speaks. He speaks with a thick Irish brogue. I love the way it sounds.

I was talking to a realtor of about three buildings on Lankershim Boulevard. It's in North Hollywood. I went and looked at them, and they were perfect for converting into a home/garage/office type of place without too much effort. All three stores were next to one another. I told them to go ahead with the conversion. They say that they can have it move-in ready ina month. That means I must go furniture hunting with Kathy for the house and the office; she is going to love that. Sometimes I get the impression that Kathy likes spending my money. That's okay. I'm happy when she's happy. I have already applied for a PI license for this state. I'm just waiting for the license to come in the mail. I hate the pictures they use for them. You always look like you're wanted, oh well.

It had been six months since I had seen Kathy. The memory I had was not a very pretty one. She was in the hospital recovering from a bullet wound in her head, and we weren't very sure she was going to make it.

Thanks to God and his infinite powers, she did recover. They couldn't take the bullet out, so she should be careful not to have too much stress. Now she is home recovering. Oh yes, one more thing. The side effect of the bullet in her head is that she has a keen sense of hearing. I must keep that in mind when I'm around her.

When I walked into her house for the first time since the accident, she opened the door, and I saw a woman that looked like an angel. She was beautiful, and I was simply happy she was alive. I walked up to her and gave her a kiss and hug. I didn't want to let her go for fear of losing her. I know it was all in my head, and I knew that, but I still worried. I didn't want her to know I was worried.

Anyway, I told her about the furniture hunting. Just like I said, she was as happy as Bogey looked when he kissed Bergman in Casablanca. I told her she could pick the furniture for the house I figured she could surprise me. I also told her that I would pick the décor of the Office. I knew what I wanted. We made a deal, she would do the house, and I would do the office and garage.   I wanted to do my office in the décor of the forties. I loved the little gate the clients had to walk through to get to my private office. They would have to pass my secretary, which of course would be Kathy. Maybe an old desk lamp with a stain glass covers one of those Tiffany covers, on the wall, there could be a picture of the old Los Angeles skyline. I always did like that kind of motif. Now I should meet with Lone Wolf and find out if he would like a job permanent with the agency. I'll meet him at his favorite bar tonight and talk to him.

I pulled up into the parking lot of 'Maxx's Place.' That's where Lone Wolf hangs out when he is not too busy on dates and riding his hog. Lone Wolf never told anyone his real name. There were only a few people besides his family that knew his real name, and I wasn't one of them. I did know he was from Pittsburg Pennsylvania and came out to Hollywood a year or two before me. He started riding motorcycles at a young age back in Pennsylvania. Harley Davidsons' bikes were his favorite or Hogs as they are known in the bike world. It has now been six months since the case had ended. I was wondering if anything changed for Lone Wolf. I wasn't sure how he was going to be. I remember when I first met him, oh, he was friendly enough but a little on the quiet side. He wasn't much for talking tostrangers. I guess I looked like a lost puppy when I spotted him at the gas station and went up to him and asked directions. Well, from that day untilnow we've become good friends. I don't know why I was nervous. I was probably paranoid. I put the best smile on my face I could conjure up andheaded inside. When I walked in and looked around, I couldn't see too well; I had to wait and let my eyes adjust to the darkness in the place.

When I was finally able to see, I saw a lot of bikers. Of course, I expected that. I mean, there were a lot of bikes in the parking lot, and this was a biker's bar. When I looked around, I spotted Lone Wolf at the end of the bar, his usual place. He had that serious look on his face, which was normal. He also had a couple of women with him, which was also normal.

They were talking. I walked up to him and asked, "Hey, do you know where I can find a beat-up old biker that might be interested in a job?"

He turned and looked at me. I don't think he recognized me at first; then a big smile came on his face. "Say It's my friend from New York. Where have you been, Sam?" He threw his arms around me and gave me a big old biker's hug then said, "I was talking about you to my friends. Heresit down, hey Joe, bring my friend a beer."

The bartender replied, "Right Lone Wolf, one beer coming up."

"Lone Wolf, did you miss me?"

"Hell yeah, what do y<u>ou</u> think? So, tell me, are you here now for good or what?"

"Well, I'll tell you I bought three storefronts on Lankershim Boulevard, and at this very moment, they are being converted into a combination Home/Office/Garage as we speak, and I'll be open for business in a couple of weeks. Are you interested in working for me full time on some cases that might come my way?"

Lone Wolf looked at me serious like for a couple of seconds and ascalm as you please, he said, "I wouldn't miss it for the world. I had morefun working with you the last time then I had had in a long time. Do you have any cases yet?"

"No, not yet. I have got to get the word out that I'm back in business. I just got my California P.I. license yesterday in the mail along with my gun permit, so I'm ready."

"Great, let's drink to that. How's Kathy doing?"

"She's doing fine. You were there with me when you heard the doctor's prognosis. I also want to thank you for looking in on her from time to time while I was gone to see if she needed anything. I'm going to take her on as my secretary. She'll be working in my new office. She'll be safe there. So, tell me, Lone Wolf, where are you working these days?"

"Good question for the moment, I'm working nowhere. I quit my job with the bank. After working with you, that job was boring." He said with a big smile.

"So, what are your plans now?"

"Well, I have enough money to last me about a year or so until I canget back on my feet."

"I'm sure you won't have to wait that long. I will need you once the business gets going."

"Well, that's good news for me."

"I'll call you in a couple of days and let you know what's happening with the office." The brought me my beer, and we talked and caught up with the chit-chat.

When I left, it was about eleven pm, and I headed home, home not being home, not yet anyway. It was Kathy and her father Mike's place in Burbank at least for another two weeks then I would be in my place boy ohboy that is going to feel great. I don't like staying in someone else's place.

TWO

Here we are just two days before the office and house open. I asked Kathy to go out with me to a nice restaurant nearby tonight to celebrate.

She said yes so, I should pick her up in about an hour. I have been at the office all day getting ready to open with last minute things that had to be done. I'm excited almost as much as Natalie Wood was in Miracle on 34th Street when Christmas had arrived, and she was waiting to see if Santa brought her the house she wanted.

I arrived at Kathy's house about fifteen minutes early. I don't like being late anywhere. I've always been that way ever since I was a kid in Brooklyn. I walked up to the door and rang the bell. A few minutes had passed, and then the door opened. There stood Kathy. I've never seen her looking lovelier, and she was wearing tight-fitting jeans, which always showed her beautiful figure and a Sky-Blue top that complimented hergreen eyes.

"Hi Sam, are you ready for me?"

I smiled and said, "I don't know if I will ever be ready for you. Youlook beautiful, as usual. I may have a problem keeping my distance."

"Good, that was my plan. Let's go eat I'm starving." Kathy closed the door, and we headed to my car. I held the door open so that Kathy could climb in, and then I went around to the driver's side and got in. I started my new car and headed down the street. I'm big on shopping for cars. I knew what I wanted, and Kathy's father knew some people that worked on cars, and he found an entirely restored nineteen-fifty-five Chevy Impala. Just what I wanted. It was a convertible, black on the outside with red seats inside just like I wanted. It has the shifter on the column, and it was automatic.

"So, where are we going to eat?" Kathy asked.

"I thought we would go to the Marina and eat at the Chart House. How does that sound?"

"Great, and how did your day go? Did you get everything done atthe office? Are you ready to open?"

"Whoa slow down too many questions at once."

Kathy laughed and said, "I'm sorry, Sam, I'm just excited about youropening. Just think about your own business. Isn't that great?"

"Yes, it is I just hope we can get the word out that we are open forbusiness so that I can get some clients."

"You will, I know it."

We arrived at the restaurant. There were a lot of people there. Theygave us a table overlooking the marina. It was beautiful. The waitress came, and we order a couple of drinks.   I   looked at Kathy's green eyes.

Whenever I looked at her, she always made me feel so complete and comfortable. I took her hands from across the table, and she stared at me. "You know, sweetheart; I missed you while I was in New York."

"Well, Sam, I don't want this to go to your head, but I missed you too. I was afraid you weren't coming back out here to live."

Sam looking surprised, said, "How could you have thought that. I told you I would be back. I'm the kind of guy who always tries to keep his promises.

"I know, 'she laughed.' I just thought it was all a dream, and whenyou left. I thought that's that."

Sam looked at her, smiled, and said, "Sometimes you say the nuttiestthings, woman. The truth of the matter is that I packed so fast,

I forgot halfof my gear. All I could think about was getting back to you. I thought of you every day."

Just then, the waiter came with our drinks and took our dinner order. When the waiter left, I looked at Kathy, and she had this big smile on herface.

"Why the big smile?"

"Oh, I'm just so happy to see you, and I'm thinking about how great it's going to be working together again. I am getting so bored just sitting athome, and besides that, my father says I'm driving him crazy."

"Wait a minute. Remember what the doctor said, no stress. You are going to be my secretary, nothing more than that at first. No running about and shooting people, remember? You're not supposed to get too excited."

Kathy's expression went from worried to naughty in a flash. "Some excitement is a good thing." She said.

I had to agree. I smiled back, "Well, yea, some excitement is good." They both started to laugh just then the waiter came over and brought the food, and the conversation stopped for a while at least.

Later, as we walked around the marina holding hands and getting reacquainted, I was feeling comfortable and at home sort of speak. At one point, we stopped and kissed. The night was covered with stars, and the moon was full without a cloud in the sky. We walked some more and looked at the docked boats. I told Kathy, "You know I've been consideringbuying a boat, not a big one, just a small one, a cabin cruiser something that we could cruise over to Catalina whenever we had time you know between cases."

"Sounds like a great idea except boats are expensive."

"Sam looked at her and said, "Yea, you're right about that, but I haveenough money from what my Aunt Gladys and my Uncle Hobart left me to buy a nice size cabin cruiser for us. Maybe down the road a way we can talkabout it again. It's getting late. We better head home, remember this is my last night at your house. Tomorrow, I move into my own home, and then you can visit me anytime."

Kathy smiled and moved closer to Sam as they walked toward the car. Sam drove Kathy back to her home.

When they went inside her father, Mike was sitting in his favorite chair, and the television was on. The funny thing was that he was sound asleep. Kathy and I smiled and laughed quietly, then Kathy spoke.

"You go on upstairs, and I'll put my father to bed. I'll see you in the morning." They kissed, and Sam headed upstairs.

Sam had a hard time sleeping. He started thinking about Margaret, his first wife, and how happy he was before the accident. Sam was worried about his relationship with Kathy, turning out the same way in a mess. He wanted it to be like any normal man. Sam wanted a woman to take care of and who will take care of him and love him as much as Sam loved her and thought Kathy would be that woman. He didn't want fate to make the same turn and end up in a dangerous place like before. He told himself he was going to have to keep the faith and have the courage that everything would work out fine. The truth is that he was scared to death. Margaret was a once in a lifetime thing. He knows that the memories of his past were getting in the way of his future. He just wished it was easy to forget his past. Only it wasn't.

THREE

The next morning both Kathy and Sam had breakfast in the kitchen while Kathy's father slept late. Sam was thinking to himself he had been looking forward to this moment, and it was finally here. There he was with his best girl in a brand-new office/home/garage and loving it.

"Tell me, Kathy, how do you like the digs?"

"Well, I love the way you have my office and your office as separatespaces. I also like the little gate that separates me from your clients when they come in. That gives it a professional look about it." We spoke for a few more minutes, and we both headed to the office for the grand opening.

The first day we had some nibbles when we had a visit from the Welcome wagon, a postman who said his cousin needed somebody to find out if his wife was cheating on him… not the kind of cases I was looking forbut today would be different I could feel it in my bones.

Sometime around two in the afternoon, a senior man walked in. He seemed to be about sixty or sixty-five years old. What got my attention was a blue cap with a familiar logo: a large white letter B on the front. There was no mistaking that logo. I felt a smile coming on. It was the old Brooklyn Dodgers baseball cap; they had played baseball at Ebbets Field in the Flatbush section of Brooklyn. This was long before they moved west and became known as the Los Angeles Dodgers. As a kid living in Brooklyn, if you followed baseball, you either were a Yankee, a Giant or a Brooklyn Dodger fan. I loved and supported the Dodgers, and my best friend at the time was mad about the

Yankees. Each of us had a favorite player they both played the same positions but for different teams. His favorite player was Mickey Mantle he played centerfield for the New York Yankees and mine was Duke Snider. He also played centerfield only for the Brooklyn Dodgers.

The gentleman came in and sat near Kathy's desk. I quickly got up and shut the door to create a professional atmosphere.

A moment later, Kathy knocked on my door, and I said, "Yes?"

Kathy opened the door, stuck her head, and said, "We have someone out there that would like to speak to you."

"Show him in." I got up to greet him and extended my hand.

"Won't you please come on in Mister…?" Kathy introduced him as Mister Charles Walters.

"Mister Walters, won't you please take a seat?" I saw him looking at my name plate on the desk.

"Thank you, Mister Ryan." He sat down and smiled and folded his hands in his lap.

I looked at him closer; he was only about five-foot-six or seven inches tall and weighed about a hundred and sixty or so pounds. He wore work shoes and a pair of jeans with a checkered shirt. He removed his hat, and I could see he had a good head of gray hair.

"Mister Walters, can we get you something to drink coffee, tea, or maybe a soda?"

"A nice cold Pepsi if you got it."

I looked at Kathy respectfully and placed an order for two cold Pepsis."

Kathy answered, "Right away, Mister, Ryan." She winked at me and scurried away.

I looked at Mister Walters and decided to break the silence with baseball. "So, tell me, Mister Walters, were you a Dodgers fan, and are you now a Los Angeles Dodger guy?"

"Are you from New York, Mister Ryan?"

"I grew up part of the time in Brooklyn and partly out here. I'vealways been a Brooklyn fan, and you?"

"Brooklyn fan too?" He had a proud smile on his face as he continued. Pointing to his cap, he said, "All my friends call me 'Cappy.' Nowadays, I follow the LA Dodgers, but they won't take the place of theold Brooklyn Dodgers as you well know."

"You're right about that. If you don't mind, I'll call you 'Cappy.'"

"Of course not; go right ahead."

"Good. Now how then can I help you?"

Just then, Kathy came in with the sodas. She placed them on the desk and left quickly as the assistant of a professional detective would do.

"Well, sir, I would like you to find my wife."

"Okay, how long has she been missing?"

He looked at me for a few seconds and then said, without a blink, "She went missing in nineteen-fifty-nine."

I was surprised. That meant he had to be about seventy-four or seventy-five years old. He didn't look at it.

After I regained my composure, I said, "That's a long time, have you tried to find her before this?"

"Yes, this will be the third time I've tried."

"What happened before?"

"They all led to dead ends. The first detective I hired looked for six months. That was about ten years ago. He came up with a woman's right name, wrong woman. The second time was about three years ago. He at least found a trail, but then it went cold. Now I'm here with you hoping you can do better than the other two." he said.

"I have an idea Cappy, why don't you start from the beginning and just tell me everything?" I took a drink from my soda, wishing there was a splash of bourbon in it and waited. I knew this was going to be a good one.

"Well, Mister Ryan, I guess it all started when I received a call from the United Artists Company. They wanted me to be a prop man for their new movie. That's what I do. I work as a Propman for the studios. I had worked in a few movies before, but nothing as big as this. It was one of my first big jobs here in Hollywood. All this took place back in nineteen-fifty-eight. I was excited about the call. I found out later the name of the moviewas "Some Like It Hot"- and the stars would be Jack Lemon and Tony Curtis with a lady you may have heard of Marilyn Monroe."

My interruption was uncontrollable, I said, "<u>You</u> worked with Marilyn Monroe?"

Cappy smiled and said, "I know, I know. Yes, she was beautiful, but she was a pain to work with. She would almost always show up late and never had her lines down. There was a rumor going around that she had sixtoes on one foot, although I don't think anyone bothered to look at her feet.Lemon and Curtis, on the other hand, always came prepared. They were real troopers, although Mr. Curtis was a bit full of himself. For all their faults, they were excellent actors, all three."

"How interesting, okay, so what happened next?"

Cappy asked, "Have you seen the movie?"

"Yes, I have, many times. I loved it."

"Then you're familiar with the all-girl band? Well, one of those girls was my future wife. You see, after I saw her on the set, I knew I just had to meet her. Later that day, when I went to eat lunch at the studio cafeteria, I saw her there. So, I walked up to her and asked her to join me. Her name was Betty Langdon. She was even more beautiful than Marilyn... five feet six and honey blonde hair. After that, we started meeting every day for lunch. We dated for about six months and got married. I was so in love with her. Still, am."

"I see, so when did she go missing?"

"Well, we got married in the fall of nineteen-fifty-eight, and she disappeared that next summer of nineteen-fifty-nine. It was shortly after the movie was released. Something extraordinary happened just before she disappeared."

"What was that?"

"The assistant director, I believe his name was Donald Strand, was found shot to death in his home. The police said they thought it was mob-related. They never found the killer. I don't think her disappearance and the murder are related, I mean, I always thought they could be, but you'd have to be a writer to tie those two threads together."

"Did Miss Langdon know the Director Mister Strand?"

"Oh, he wasn't the Director he was the Assistant Director Ye, we alldid. He was always on the set. He got along with everybody. You know, like most men in show business, he was a womanizer."

"Did Miss Langdon go out with Mister Strand, before you I mean?" I could tell by the look on his face he didn't believe what he was about to say.

"Yes, I think they went out once or twice before we started dating."

"Did Miss Langdon get along with everyone on the set?"

"Oh yea, everybody liked Betty. She was always smiling and jokingin between takes. She could do a great imitation of Marilyn. Even Marilynlaughed every time Betty did it on the set."

"Anything else you can remember?"

"Well, I remember shortly after the release of the movie, Betty started coming home late, and sometimes, she would say she was going out to the movies with her girlfriends and then be out late. I used to get worriedabout that and would tell her so."

"What did she say when you told her that?"

"She would smile, that smile she always gave me when Betty didn't want me to worry then she would say, don't worry about me. I can take care of myself."

The look on his face drew a red flag from me. I had been in the business for a long time, and I could always tell when something was a little hinky, and this was it. I rose and shook Cappy's hand, continuing.

I said, "Okay, Cappy, I think I have enough to get started. Please stop by Kathy's desk on the way out. She'll give you our rates, and you will have to sign some agreement paperwork, then you can give her a retainer along with your address and a phone number where we can reach you. If you agree with the rates and still want me to take the case, tell Kathy, and I'll start on it tomorrow."

"Thank you, Mister Ryan. I hope you will be able to do what no one else has."

"We'll probably have a lot more questions once we get into this. I'llgive you a call in about a week. How does that sound, Cappy?"

Mister Walters turned on his way out and said, "That'll be fine, Mister Ryan that will be just fine. Thank you very much for taking an interest in my dilemma."

He closed the door, and I was alone again but not for long. After about a minute or so, Kathy knocked and opened the door with a smile on her face. She had the five hundred dollars fanned out in her hand.

"Well, the first case we are on our way. Isn't this exciting?"

"Yes, it is, except something is bothering me about our Mister Walters I just can't put my finger on it. Anyway, now I'll need you to do a background check on Mister Walters and Betty Langdon, okay? Also, see if you can get the name of anyone who worked on the movie with them and see if they are still alive. We'll need to talk to them. Also, put that money in the office safe. We may need it later."

Kathy looked at me very seriously like and said, "Right away, boss," and she saluted me then turned and left. I smiled. Kathy told me that our computers would arrive tomorrow sometime.

They would put a desktop computer on her desk and one on mine. The printer would be in her office. That way, she could keep up with the paperwork better.

I sat there for a while I was trying to replay everything in my head that Mister Walters had told me. I couldn't put my finger on it, but something didn't jive. I remember reading somewhere not too long ago that the Mob had tried to get a foot in the door in the Entertainment Industry, but I thought that was back when they found Bugsy Segal shot dead in the head in his Hollywood home. I think that was back in the middle forties. I wonder if they were trying again in the fifties. It was four-thirty. I told Kathy to start a folder on the case, and she could put it on the computer tomorrow when they set them up.

"Kathy, do you know a place close by we could eat supper?"

"Yes, as a matter of fact, I do. There is Bob's Big Boy down the street on Lankershim. Their prices are reasonable, and the food was good too."

"Great, get ready, and we'll close up shop and go."

A few minutes later, we were in the car headed toward Big Boys. There wasn't much difference with the traffic here, and in New York, except out here, it seems to spread out more so than in New York. Los Angeles area was comprised of many cities near it. There was Hollywood, Burbank, North Hollywood, and West Hollywood and a few others. It was hard to tell where one ended, and another began, but that was LA.

FOUR

What I like best out here are the parking lots. Unlike New York, there's almost always space. We arrived at the restaurant in about fifteen minutes and were parked and seated shortly after that.

We went inside and took a seat by the window. Show business was all over this town, and I didn't want to miss it when it walked by. As a part-time actor, I never know when I might run into somebody, I might end up auditioning. I played the role of a detective well, and there were Movie studios and casting agents everywhere. There were ordinary people there, but you could never be sure who you might meet. The system was more stringent too, I remember in New York; you didn't need an agent, to get ajob, out here the studios wouldn't even talk to you unless you are signed with an agent, the agents knew that, and they were very picky who they hired. They didn't believe your resumes. They always wanted to see a video of what you did. That way, they could see how you worked in frontof a camera.

The waiter came over and took our order. While we waited for our food, Kathy and I chatted. I loved listening to Kathy. She could make a grocery store run seem like a big adventure. I often pictured us as Clark Gable and Claudette Colbert in "It Happened One Night," an epic regarding banter and foreplay.

"So, tell me, Sam, are you going to keep up with the acting side of your enterprise in-between cases?"

"You know I would like it too, but I haven't had time to think aboutit, but that sounds like an appealing option. I mean I do have a SAG card. That reminds me I should get in touch with SAG and give them my newaddress. They still have the old one in New York."

Kathy smiled and said, "I can do that for you when I get to the office in the morning."

I smiled, knowing I didn't have to explain the Screen Actors Guildacronym or its significance to Kathy. Then I moved on to the topic of the day.

"Were you able to find anything about our client and his wife?"

"Not really," she said and continued with, "I figured I would consider it tomorrow when we get the computers in the office. In themeantime, what do you think of the way I furnished your house?"

"I love it. You did a great job. It already has that lived-in look. I especially like the four-poster bed. You think we'll have time to try it out sometime soon?"

She gave me one of those smiles I've come to love and said, "I don'tsee why not; this weekend would be a good time as any."

"Not as good as tonight would be, but it sounds like a plan. Nowabout this case, you do know that it's going to be a pretty cold one."

"Yeah, but if anyone can heat it, you can," she said.

Sam speaks, "Oh, by the way, I got in touch with Lone Wolf yesterday, and he said he was looking forward to working with us again. I need to call him in the morning and let him know we have a case. He'll beglad to hear that."

Kathy smiled and said, "I almost forgot about him. I'm glad he'll be on board for this one. He has this city wired. He'll be a lot of help when we start looking for the people we need to track down."

Just then, the waiter came by with the food, and we dug in. It turns out; we were just as hungry as I thought we would be. Maybe it was all thetalk about the four-poster bed. Afterward, I dropped Kathy in Burbank. I kissed her politely at the door and resigned myself to the fact that my first night at the new house would be alone.

When I drove into my new garage, I got out and stood there a moment looking the place over. I felt comfortable with the idea I belonged there now, and I was looking forward to an exciting road ahead.

I woke up the next morning much later than I had anticipated. I was hoping to get an early start and be at the office by nine, but when I shot my first panicky glance at the clock, it said nine-thirty a.m., and I jumped out of bed and took a fifteen-second shower. Alright, so it was a fifteen-minute shower. I was still dazed but trying to look in control when I headed out of the house at 10 a.m. Good thing I had a short walk through the garage to my office. Kathy was already sitting there waiting for the computer technician to come.

I greeted Kathy with a smile, saying, "Good morning, sweetie, what time did you get here?"

Kathy turned and smiled, saying, "Good morning, lazybones. I got anearly start at about seven or so. I know you're the boss, but ten a.m.?" She started laughing.

"I guess I was more wiped out than I thought. Did I miss anything?"

"Not really; there was one call from the computer people. They said their man was on his way."

"Good. Make sure we get all the programs we asked for; on the computer, we can't count on me when it comes to computers. Oh, by the way, Kathy, did you have those business cards made?"

"Yes, I did they said they would be here sometime today. I hope you like the design. I also called the Post Office and found out Betty Langdon's last known address was on Lankershim Boulevard just past Sherman Way. It was an apartment complex, but that was back in nineteen-seventy-five. I'm still trying to get her current address."

"What about her work history? Do we have anything on that yet?"

"Well, I called the SAG office to see if she's still an active member. She is. I also gave them your change of address."

"What about an agent? Is she listed with one?"

"If she did have one, SAG didn't have a listing."

"Let me get a cup of coffee, and then I'll drive to her old address and see if I can find anything out."

An hour later, I arrived at Ms. Langdon's last known address-perhaps a decade too late to catch up on her or anyone who ever knew her. My morning office time was brief; the only mail I had to sort through, was addressed to "Dear Occupant," and I felt it would be outrageous to ask my gorgeous secretary for more than one cup coffee when I had had ample time to wake up before I showed my face at work.

When I got to the apartment, I found a parking space close to the office. I parked the car and noticed another car parked nearby. It was a four-door ford, black in color, as the cops like to say. A gentleman was sitting at the wheel. He had black hair; I couldn't see him very well. I took a mental note of the plate number. I wasn't sure why the man was watching me, but past experiences told me I should follow up. It's the gut feeling that gets you out of trouble, so maybe this one would help avoid it altogether.

When I entered the office, the woman sitting at the desk looked up and smiled. She looked to be in her late thirties with brown hair below her shoulders. She was neatly dressed in a pant-suit dark blue.

"Hello, can I help you, sir?"

"Yes, I'm looking to find out some information about a past tenant of yours, Ms. Langdon."

"What is her first name?"

"Betty. I think she was living here until nineteen-seventy-seven, but I'm not sure of the date. I'm hoping you have a forwarding address for her?"

"Who are you, sir?" The woman inquired.

Sam is a little taken aback by the question of not thinking that the information he was looking for was an invasion of privacy. Those records are usually on file for the public to see unless it is company policy. He says, "I am Ryan, Sam Ryan, I'm a private investigator."

"Ms. Betty Langdon… hmm… let me look." She went to a file cabinet and started rifling through some folders. After a few moments, she took out a file folder and carried it to her desk and continued to read.

"Betty Langdon. Yes, she was here from March of nineteen-sixty, and then she and her daughter moved out in nineteen-seventy-six. No forwarding address." She looked at me and said, "That's all I have."

"Do you know what the daughter's name is or how old her daughter was when they moved?"

"Well, her name was Marilyn, and as far as her age, I didn't feel it was my business to ask. But looking at her, I would say strictly as a guess you understand, that she looked to be in her early to middle teens, maybe fourteen or so. The girl was born while they lived in the apartment. I remember her mother saying something about moving north, but she never said where."

"Did she have many visitors while she was here?"

"I started working here in the spring of nineteen-seventy-five. I didn't know Marilyn her that well. We don't make it a policy of snooping on our tenants unless they are troublemakers, and as I remember, she and her daughter kept pretty much to themselves. Although, I do remember they liked to lay out by the pool a lot. If the tenants aren't raising hell and partying all the time, we didn't keep tabs. But she had some women folks that visited from time to time. Like I said before, she and her daughter kept pretty much to themselves."

I thanked her and turned to leave when she stopped me dead in my tracks, saying, "She did leave an emergency name and number if you're interested?"

"Yes, I would be interested." Sam was glad she found something and continued. "I knew I could count on you!"

"It says here you can contact a Miss Agnes Martin at Three-Ten-Five-Five-Five-Three-Two-Seven-Eight."

I started writing it down as I spoke, "Thank you, is that all?"

"Yes, that's all I have in her folder. I'm afraid." I thanked her and went out to the parking lot, and I got in my car.

The black ford was still there, but the driver was absent. Maybe my hunch was wrong. I drove back to the office. When I walked inside, a short, skinny guy was installing a big bulky computer on Kathy's desk.

Kathy refrained from her usual greeting, a kiss—at least on the cheek—and asked if I had any luck at the apartment complex.

"Yes, as a matter of fact," I said. "I see the computer man showed up."

"Yes! He has yours up and running, and he's finishing up mine now. I can't wait to try it out."

"Good I have this license plate number for you. See if you can find aname and address for it. Also, here is a name and phone number I want you to try her name and number. It's on this piece of paper. I'll be in my office." Sam drops the piece of paper on Kathy's desk and turns toward his office.

"Okay, Sam will do."

I had been sitting at my desk for about twenty minutes when Kathy buzzed me on the intercom and informed me that a Miss Agnes Martin wason the line. Kathy said my first caller of the day, and she sounded a bit defensive.

"Okay, I'll take it from here." Sam clicked the button of the line the woman was on.

"Hello?"

"Hello. I'm Agnes Martin, who am I speaking to?"

"Hello, my name is Sam Ryan. I'm calling on behalf of Charles Walters."

"I see. Are you a lawyer?"

"No, I am not. I'm a private detective. I'm calling because I'm trying to locate Mrs. Betty Walters. She is married to Charles Walters. He's been looking for her for some time. He hired me to find her if I could. You're my first lead. Like I said before, my name is Sam Ryan, and I'm a private detective. Do you happen to know where she is now?"

"Well, I'll tell you, Mister Ryan, the last time I spoke to her was back in the summer of nineteen and seventy-six."

"I understand, Ms. Martin, but I still think you might be able to help. May I come over to your place and ask you a few questions?"

"Is she in any trouble?"

"No, we're just trying to locate her."

There was silence on the other end. I knew she was trying to make up her mind as to help me or not, then she continued, "I work at Denny's restaurant in Sherman Oaks. I get off at five this afternoon. We can talk then if you like."

"That sounds good. Thank you very much for your time. Ms. Martin. I'll meet you outside Denny's, and maybe we could go for somecoffee at the establishment of your choice."

After I hung up, I noticed the computer guy was gone. "Well. Kathy, how do you like the new computers?"

"It's going take a little time to get used to, but it will help a lot," shesaid picking up a thick book, she continued, "Looks like it's going to take some reading too. But I did call the DMV about the plate number you gaveme, and they said they would get back with me if not today tomorrow, for sure. I entered all the information for our first client. That way, we would have a record of our first meeting."

"Great. It will probably take you a week to get through that manifesto of a computer manual. In the meantime, I'm going to see Ms. Martin at five, and I'd like to come back and pick you up for dinner afterward. How does that sound?"

"You <u>do</u> know how to make a woman happy, Sam." She was laughing when I headed out the door.

FIVE

Driving over to speak to Ms. Martin, I was thinking to myself, and this is going to be an exciting conversation. She may or may not be able to help me. I looked into the rearview mirror and noticed the car following melooked pretty much like the same car that was in that apartment lot on Lankershim earlier today. I kind of indirectly kept an eye on him while I was driving. I noticed when I made a right turn, and he made a right turn too. Yep, he was following me, alright. I'll keep an eye on him and see if he follows me to Denny's.

I pulled into the parking lot of Denny's and parked. I walked around to the front entrance, and a woman was standing there. She looked to be approximately sixty and about five-foot-four or five. We both looked at each other but didn't say anything.

Finally, I smiled and asked, "Ms. Martin?"

She nodded and said, "Yes, Mister Ryan?"

I said yes, and then we shook hands. "Shall we go inside, and I'll buy us some coffee." When we turned to go inside, I took a quick look at the entrance of the parking lot. That same black car was coming into the lot. I didn't want to bother Ms. Martin with my situation, so I didn't say anything as we went inside.

"I don't know how much help I'll be."

I looked at her and said, "Well, let's just see what happens."

We went inside, and some of her co-workers said hello as we sat at a booth. I made a point of facing the door, so I could see if that man walked in. I was beginning to feel like I was in one of those black and white movies from the forties.

The Waitress came over and spoke, "What's the matter can't getenough of this place, Agnes?"

She just smiled and said, "I guess so, how about a couple of coffees." She looked over at me and said, "Cream and sugar?"

"Yes, please, thank you."

"Do you mind if I called you Agnes? It would make our conversation a little easier."

"I don't mind sure it's no problem."

"Good, and you may call me Sam. Okay, why don't you tell me what you know about Betty Langdon?"

"Well, I don't know where to begin, so I'll start by saying I have known Betty for about let me see, yes, about twenty-years. She was fun to know her when she was living in those apartments on Lankershim."

"Did she tell you she was married?"

"Not at first, after about a month, we were talking one day, and it just came out. The only thing she said was that she was married, but she wasn't living with her husband. She also mentioned that she had a three-year-old daughter named Marilyn. She was timid in those early days. She didn't want to say too much. She looked afraid all the time. Whenever I would ask her if there were anything wrong, she would shrug it off and say; I don't want to talk about it right now."

"Did she ever tell you why she was afraid, or what she was afraid of?"

"Not exactly, I think it was around the third month. We were both working together at Denny's I helped to get her that job. We were on our lunch hour, and she said that she was hiding from her husband. I said, why was he abusing you? She came right back with no that wasn't it. She said I love him. I'm trying to keep him safe. I did something terrible, and I can't go back to him yet."

"Did she ever tell you why she was running?" At that question, Agnes looked as though she knew the answer but wasn't sure if she should tell me. At that precise moment, I looked at the door, and I saw a dark-haired gentleman come in alone. He could have been the same one that followed me here. But I wasn't sure. I looked back at Mrs. Martin; she hadthat confused look on her face. So, I said, "Continue what were you going to say."

"Well, I was going to say she started crying and went into the restroom, so I followed to see if I could help her. She was upset. She asked our boss if she could go home. Betty said she didn't feel well. She eventually told me she was having an affair with the Assistant Director of the movie she was working on at the time."

"Did she tell you his name?"

"Yes, wait a minute I'll think of it... yes... yes, I remember, it was a Mister Strand. Yes, that's it, Donald Strand. She said he was very good looking. She said he was murdered, and she saw it."

What she just told me makes this case a whole lot more interesting, now if I could only locate Betty.

"Did you see her after that day?"

"Yes, a couple of times but never talked again about Mister Strand. The last time I saw her was… let me see yes about August of seventy-six."

"Can you think of anything else that might help me to find her?"

"She talked about a brother one time and a girlfriend named Coleen. I gathered that they got along pretty good from the way she talked about him."

"Did she say where he was living?"

"She did mention somewhere north of here. Yes, yes, in Newhall. That's about fifteen or twenty miles north of here."

"Great; I appreciate your help. Thank you very much for seeing me."

"No problem, if you need anything else, I'll be here at Denny's."

I got up, turned, and headed for the door. Mrs. Martin stopped me and said, "I hope Marilyn is okay."

"So, do I? I'll let you know."

When I got outside, I looked around for that black car that was following me. I didn't see it, so I figured that it had already left. I was wondering when I would see him again. I headed back to the office.

When Sam entered the office, the man that followed him stood across the street from the office and observed. He saw Sam talking to Kathy at her desk. The man was trying to figure out how to explain to Samthe true nature of his visit. He decided the best way was to meet with Sam face to face and tell him. He walked across the street to Sam's office and went inside.

Sam and Kathy stopped talking and turned as a gentleman dressed in a dark suit with an open button light-colored shirt entered the office. Sam smiled and said, "Hello, how can we help you?"

The man walked toward Sam and said with a compelling smile, "I believe I'm the one that can help you." He continued, "My name is Ed Hawkins, and I represent the Allied Insurance Company."

"Well, I'm sorry, but we are not interested in any Insurance now."

The man laughed and said, "That's good because I'm not trying to sell you any."

"Okay, back to my original question, how can we help you?"

"Sir, I think I'll be able to help you. I happen to know you're looking for a Miss Betty Langdon correct?"

"Could be you're right we have a client that is looking for her. What about it?"

"I hope your client's name isn't Mister Walters."

Now Sam is curious he is beginning to wonder what kind of game the gentleman is playing.

"What interests do you have in this case?"

"Well, if your client's name is Mister Walters, then we might have a problem."

"And why would that be a problem?"

"Well, sir, Mister Walters is dead. He died a couple of years ago back in nineteen-seventy-nine. I'm trying to locate his wife a Betty Langdon, assuming she took her maiden name. I wanted to give her a life insurance policy left to her by her husband. It's for two million dollars."

Sam turns and looks at Kathy and then turns back and looks at Mister Hawkins and says, "Well, sir, why don't you come in and tell me the whole story." Sam turns and walks into his office, and Mister Hawkins follows behind and closes the door.

Sam is now sitting at his desk. He looks at Mister Hawkins for a moment and then says, "Won't you please sit, would you like some coffee or a soda?"

"No, thank you, Mister Ryan."

Sam was anxious to start the questioning, "Okay, let's start with thisquestion, do you have a picture of Mister Walters?"

Mister Hawkins reaches for his briefcase and opens it while saying, "As a matter of fact, I do have one picture. It is the only picture we could obtain that shows them both. Mr. Hawkins shows the picture. After they were married, the picture showed up. We had a flag set up in our databaseto let us know if a Mister Walters showed up anywhere in town. It went off when you put Mister Walters on your computer as a client. The flag went upin our database."

Sam looks at the picture and says, "If this is Mister Charles Walters in this picture, then, who was that man that came into our office the other day claiming <u>he</u> was Mister Walters?"

Mister Hawkins speaks, "I'm sure I don't know, but what I do knowis that wasn't Mister Walters."

Sam pages Kathy on the intercom and says, "Kathy did that computer man put all the programs in our computer we requested when he was here the other day?"

"Yes, Sam, he did. Why?"

"Good, then do me a favor. Get a picture from the surveillance camera we had set up. And run the facial recognition program and see if it tells us who the man was."

"Right away, Sam."

Sam looks back at Mister Hawkins and continues, "I'm glad we had an in-house video camera running at the time. We'll get this problem aired out quick."

Mr. Hawkins stands and says, "Good in the meantime, Mister Ryan. I'll leave my card with you in case you need to contact me." He hands the card to Sam. Sam approaches Kathy and speaks, "Say, Kathy, did you get that video picture of our Mr. Walters yet?"

Kathy replies, "Yes, it's printing out now."

"Well, let's have a look at it before you run it through the computer." Kathy walks over to the printer and gets the picture and hands it to Sam, who is standing with Mr. Hawkins.

Kathy speaks to Mr. Hawkins, "You will have to excuse the slowness of this procedure you see we just opened for business about a week ago, and the people from the computer company just set our system up, and we're still learning it."

Sam looked at the picture said, "Hmm, I thought there was something strange about him. Okay, run it through our computer and see what comes up. Before giving it to Kathy, he shows it to Mr. Hawkins. Mr. Hawkins looked at it for a moment and then spoke.

"I believe I know this man he works for a crime family in New Jersey. I think his name is Frank Rampulla. He works as a hitman for the Cariola, crime family."

"Are you serious?

"To make sure we all are on the same page, run this picture, Kathy, and see what we come up with." He hands it to Kathy.

"Right, boss, I'll do it right now." She heads back toward her deskwhile still talking, "By the way, I found someone that worked with Betty on that movie. He worked the lights on the movie; his name is Ben Wright. I put his name and address and phone number on your desk."

Sam replies, "Great; I'll make a call and see if he's going to be there for a while."

"Well, I think I'm finished here, for now, I'm going to leave. Youhave my card if anything comes up that you have to talk to about." Mr. Hawkins walks out, and Sam goes into his office and dials the number that Kathy just gave him and waits for an answer.

After the second ring, someone picks up, and Sam speaks, "Hello, who am I speaking to?" Samputs it on the speakerphone so that he could hear it better.

"Hello, this is Ben Wright, who am I talking to?"

Sam replies, "Mr. Wright, my name is Sam Ryan, I'm a Private Detective, and I'm looking for the whereabouts of a Mrs. Betty Langdon." Sam could tell that Mr. Wright thought before he spoke.

"That's a name out of the past. I haven't heard that name for years. Why are you looking for her?"

"Well, I'm trying to locate her for a client of ours. I want to talk toyou in person if I may. I must do so now."

"Well… I'll be here for the next couple of hours if you like you could come over now."

"Great, where are you located? I mean, what is your address?"

"I live just about a block from Grumman's Theatre in Hollywood. The address is forty-two-twenty Hollywood Blvd."

Sam speaks, "Great; I'll be there within the hour."

"Fine, I'll be waiting." There is a click on the other end of the call asBen hangs up the phone.

After hanging up the phone, Sam gets up from behind his desk and heads out toward Kathy's office to let her know what's up.

Kathy speaks first, "I have a name for the face of our first client. He suspected of killing that Assistant Director of 'Some Like It Hot,' Donald Strand by the police."

Sam turns toward Kathy, "When I spoke to Miss Martin yesterday, she said that Betty Langdon told her that she was a witness to that same murder. She was having an affair with Mr. Strand at the time."

Sam stops at her desk and says, "Okay, so tell me his name already. We don't have time for games."

Kathy replies, "Keep your shirt on, Mr. Hawkins is correct. His name is Frank Rampulla, and they have his address listed as Lodi New Jersey."

Okay, great work. Now listen, I'm going to visit Ben Wright and see if he can tell us anything worthwhile."

With that, he then heads toward the door to the garage. He climbs in the car and opens the garage door with the remote. He starts the engine and moves out the door and makes a right on the street.

The traffic on the freeway this time of the day is not too bad. He heads south and exits at the Capitol Records building in Hollywood. He goes down to Sunset Boulevard and turns right. Now the traffic is heavy. It always is in Hollywood. It's the right time of the year for tourists. There are also all kinds of bus tours. As he passes the Grumman's Theatre, he sees a lot of tourists looking to see if their feet fit into any of the old moviestars' footprints in front of the Theatre. He remembers when he was there, he checked his hands against the stars' prints that were there. His hands matched those of Clark Gable. He laughed as the red light brought him back to reality. Now all he should do is find a parking spot. Good luck with that one. He turns right two blocks passed the Theatre and went up one block where the homes start. Hollywood only really has two famous main streets, Hollywood and Sunset Boulevards going East and West, andVine Street going North and South. Sam finally finds a parking space and parks. He gets out of the car and heads toward the address on Hollywood Boulevard. After a few moments, Sam finds himself in front of 4220. Herings the doorbell. A minute later, he hears a man's voice through the speaker on the wall. "Yes, who is it?"

Sam speaks, "It's me, Sam Ryan. I spoke to you on the phone." Thebuzzer sounds, and the door unlocked and opened. There is a long hallway, and Sam heads down the hall waiting for one of the doors to open. It just dawns on him he never asked what apartment number it was. Only then, anentry in front of him opens, and a wheelchair pulls out. A senior man with a lot of gray hair is sitting in a wheelchair. It's kind of difficult to tell how tall a person is when he is sitting, but this gentleman looked to be about six feet and on the thin side. He waves with a smile and says, "Come on in."

Sam walks into the apartment and closes the door behind him. There is a short hallway, and it opens to a living room.

Ben speaks first. "Here, Mr. Ryan, please sit over here; it's a more comfortable chair." Sam walks over and sits.

"Thank you, Mr. Wright.

He looks around the apartment. There is one of those old fireplaces with a high mantle across the top. On the mantel are an Oscar and a Grammy. Sam is impressed. He has never met anyone that had won any awards like those before. Secretly he had hoped to win one someday. "Nice awards, did you receive them recently?"

Ben smiles and answers, "Oh no, those are from many years ago a time long gone." Then to change the subject, he says, "So tell me how I can help you? You said you were looking for Betty?"

"Yes, we have a client that says Mrs. Langdon had been missing for about twenty years."

Ben looked a little surprised and bewildered as he spoke. "She hasn't been missing just in hiding. She witnessed a murder back in let me see it was just after we wrapped 'Some Like It Hot.' That would have been about nineteen-sixty."

Sam speaks, "How did you know all that?"

"Well, I met Betty shortly after she landed the part of a female bandmember in the movie. I was working on the lights for that movie. Along about the second day, she started asking me all kinds of questions about Marilyn Monroe and the other stars. For some reason, she thought I knewabout the stars. I mean by then, I had been in the business for about five years, so I guess I did know a little. She was like a little girl in a candy shop. Always excited about everything. She wasn't afraid of anything. I remember the first day on the set Tony, you know Tony Curtis saw her and started flirting with her. She put him in his place straight away. After that, he gave her plenty of space."

"So, tell me, when was the last time you saw her?"

"Saw her; I haven't seen her since the end of shooting the movie. But she called me about two years ago. I knew she was married to Charles Walters. He worked props for the shoot. What I don't understand is what she saw in him, but that's another story. She was beautiful, and it was love at first sight. They married about six months into shooting. Why would she leave him? Am I sure I don't know? I do know at the time there was a rumor going around; she was seen with the AD Donald Strand. But I didn't believe it. Then shortly after filming was over, they found Mr. Strand dead at his place with a bullet hole in his head. That's when she disappeared.

When I spoke to her a couple of years ago, I asked her why she ran, that's when Betty told me she saw Donald get shot and Betty was scared, so she ran. Betty had had a girl by her then-husband Charles and named her after Marilyn Monroe. When I spoke to her a couple of years ago, she told me by then her daughter was about seventeen or eighteen. I'm not sure."

Sam speaks, "Did she give you her address?"

"No, I told her I had spoken to her husband a couple of years earlier and that he was still looking for her. He was sick then. I heard that he died a little bit later after I had seen him. I told her so. I could tell by her voice that she was distraught. That was the last time I heard from her."

Sam looked at Ben; he wanted to know a little more about him, so he asked. "Ben, hope you don't mind me asking, but how did you end up in that chair."

Ben just smiled and said, "Oh, this is temporary. At least that's what the doctors tell me. I was setting up the lights for a shot we were trying to get for this movie I was working on. Oh, it must have been a couple of months ago, and the lights fell on my legs and crushed the lower part of my body. The doctor said he could fix me up. He said that he would have me walking in no time. Well, that was six months ago. Here I sit waiting.

Sam is trying to make Ben feel better and replies: "Well, that's good news. Just hang in there, and it will happen, I'm sure. I thank you for your time and remember to do what the doctors say, and you will be out of that chair in no time." Sam turns to leave, and Ben stops him.

"Do me a favor if you see Betty tell her I was asking for her. She's a great girl."

"Sure thing, I will do that. See you." Sam turns to leave.

"Wait, you didn't tell me what you are going to do?"

Sam smiles and says as he leaves, "Keep on looking, of course."

Sam enters the street and notices that there are a lot of people around. He chalks it up to tourists. He gets in his car and heads back.

It was late when Sam returned to the office. When he walked in, he could see Kathy deep in thought with the computer manual and then at the computer like she was comparing the two. She was getting used to the new desktop computer. She looked like she was having fun. Sam says, "Let's go eat I'm starving. Where do you want to go?"

Kathy looked up from the computer and said, "Yeah, sure I'm hungry too. I feel like Italian. What about you?"

Sam replies, "Sounds like the Olive Garden to me. Let's go."

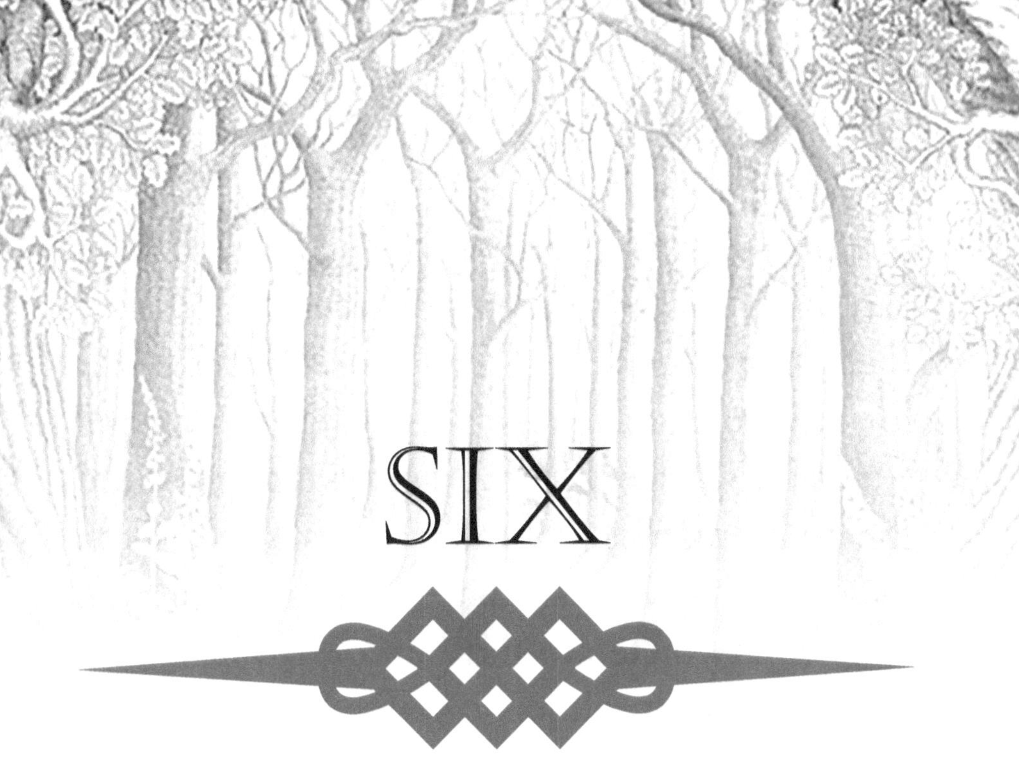

SIX

After we ate, I suggested a walk by the boats at the Piers in Marina Del Rey. I love looking at the boats at night. You could see the sun settingon the ocean and all the sailboats on the docks starting to light up from the people living on board their vessels. Kathy was up to it. I had heard a lot about the place, and I thought it would be nice to spend some time there. When we finally found a parking space, we walked to the docks, fortunately, we only had to go a block up and one block over to get there.

We went out onto the docks and started walking to the other end. I think it was about half a mile to the other end. It's a great place to go on a date. I love being around Kathy. She always makes me feel like I don't have a care in the world. She also makes me feel like I could do anything. That's an excellent gift for a woman to have. No matter how strong a manfeels, I feel like the right woman around the right man is unbeatable qualities. When you find that woman that makes you feel that way when you're around her, don't let her go. We held hands while we walked. I could feel my feelings coming back the way I felt before Kathy's accident. We stopped and looked into each other's eyes. We kissed, and time stood still.

Kathy spoke first, "You know, Sam, when I'm around you, I feel thisis where I'm supposed to be. I feel well whenever I'm with you; you make me feel complete."

Sam looked at Kathy. First, he said nothing. Sam just looked into hereyes. Finally, he said, "You remember when you were shot, all I could think about was that it was my fault. I was so sorry that I let you work on that case with me.

Then while you were in the hospital recovering from your wound, I thought how lucky I was that God spared you for me to love forever. Now that we're together, I don't want us ever to be apart."

Kathy looked back at Sam and put her arm in his and said, "Sam let's go to your place. I want to lie next to you. I want to feel your body next to mine. I love you, and I want to show you just how much." With that, she kissed Sam, and they both turned and headed back to the car.

When Kathy awoke the next morning, she was lying next to Sam. He was still sleeping, and Kathy was watching him. Sam looked so relaxed and comfortable. His eyes opened, and the first thing he saw was Kathy. A big smile came across his face, and he spoke, "Good morning, sweetheart. I just had the most wonderful dream. But now that I'm completely awake and lying next to you, I'm not so sure it was a dream. It was too good to be a dream. You know it's true what they say about truth being stranger than fiction." He put his arms around Kathy and kissed her with the feeling of a man that never wanted it to end.   T h e atmosphere was mutual with Kathy, and the love cycle started all over again.

Later in the day, Sam was driving up toward Newhall on Interstate 14. He was still thinking about Kathy, but also, he couldn't help but notice how beautiful the scenery was. No wonder so many people were moving from the East Coast to the West Coast. He turned right onto the exit that turned into San Fernando Valley Rd. and headed toward the town of Newhall. Another thought came into Sam's head. He thought him, and Kathy doesn't know much about Mr. Rampulla. Sam was also pretty sure that he was the one that shot the director Mr. Strand, and he thought he could only prove that if he could find Mrs. Langdon alive. Sam mentally reminds himself to talk to Kathy about this when Sam got back.

When Sam got to Lyons Avenue, he made a left turn per the instructions Kathy gave him. Sam was wondering why he does the things he does. Sam has always cared about people. Sam has always wanted the best for them. If they needed help, he wanted to be able to give them support.

He pulled up in front of the address Fourteen Lyons Ave. I parked the car and got out. He went on up to the door, knocked, and waited for a reply. After a minute, the door opened, and there stood a gentleman about six-foot-tall gray hair and on the slim side.

The man spoke, "Yes, sir, can I help you?"

Sam replied, "Yes, my name is Sam Ryan. I'm a private investigator, and I am looking for Betty Langdon. I understand she is your sister, and I'd like to speak to her if she's home."

Man, in the doorway, was wondering what the private investigator wanted with his sister. "Has she done something wrong?"

"No, she hasn't done anything wrong that I'm aware of, I have a few questions for her. Is she in?"

The man in the doorway has a suspicious look on his face and answers, "Well, she's not here now can I give her a message?"

Sam hands him one of the business cards that Kathy had given him before he left the office. She was right he did like the design, "Here's mycard can you please have her call me when she gets in, it is of great importance. Oh, by the way, I didn't get your name."

"Sure, thing Mister Ryan. My name is Larry Langdon."

Sam turns and walks back to the car and leaves. When Sam getsback to the office, Kathy is waiting with a smile on her face.

Sam speaks, "well, Kathy, why the smile?"

"Well, I finally got through the computer manual at least getting to know the things I need to know to get started, and it's going to make a great reference guide when I need to find out something about the computer."

"Kathy, did our client leave a forwarding address and phone number for us to reach him if we found out anything about his 'wife'?"

Kathy speaks, "Yes, he did, and the address he left with us is in West Hollywood about a block from the Capitol Record Building."

Just about that time, the front door opened and in walked Lone Wolf. "Hey, Sam, Kathy, how are you guys doing?" He looked around and continued talking, "This is a great place you got here."

Kathy ran toward Lone Wolf and hugged him, hello saying, "Lone Wolf it's good to see you."

"Good to see you guys too, Sam tells me we got us a case a good one."

Sam speaks, "It's a good one, alright." He turns to Kathy and speaks, "Kathy, I'm going to show Lone Wolf the rest of the place, be back in five."

"Lone Wolf, c' mon, I'll show you around the place and tell you all about the case."

They both headed toward the door to the garage. Sam opens the door, and they both go out into the garage and close the door. Kathy goes back to work. Lone Wolf stopped dead in his tracks. He was staring at the car that Sam had parked there. He had not seen it before. Lone Wolf speaks first, "I like this car you have. Did you restore the car yourself?"

"No, Kathy's father knew someone that worked on all kinds of cars. He did a pretty good job on it, though. I must say I am very pleased with it."

"I'll say you don't see too many 56' Chevy convertibles in this good a shape. I like the color. Of course, you do know that the cops are more likely to stop you then someone else because of that color."

"No, no, you're confused that only stop you quicker if the exterior is red, not the exterior. I know, but that might come in handy in my line of work." He winks then smiles at Lone Wolf.

Lone Wolf smiles back and laughs, saying, "Okay, so tell me about this new case we're doing."

"Well, to begin with, this guy comes into my office about a week ago and tells me he is looking for his wife. It seems that she had been missing since nineteen-sixty-one and he wanted me to find her. Then a couple of days ago I find out that this guy is not her husband but some hitman that shot and killed some director named Donald Strand back in nineteen-fifty-nine. He supposedly was the AD on the movie 'Some Like It Hot.' The woman we are looking for Ms. Langdon was in the movie, and she was having an affair with the AD. Betty's married name is Mrs. Walters. The hitman was looking to find her. Betty was an eyewitness to the killing of Donald Strand, the AD on the movie. She had been hiding in the bathroom at the time of the shooting, and he found out later that she saw the whole thing, and he wanted to tie up loose ends. Betty has been in hiding since nineteen-sixty-one."

"Sam, you haven't been out here for very long, and you are already talking like you were born here. What is AD?"

Sam speaks with a smile and says, "Well, I wasn't born here. You're right, but I do know that an AD means an Assistant Director. I think I'm going to pick up a lot of new words and phrases. That's an occupational hazard."

"Boy, oh boy, this sounds like something that is right up your alley. What do you want me to do?"

"Funny you should ask I have an address I would like you to checkout in West Hollywood. It supposed to be where our hitman Frank Rampulla might be staying."

Lone Wolf speaks, "This guy sounds pretty dangerous. You know I'm ready and willing to help with this case. But remember, I don't have a gun like you. What if he starts shooting at me?"

"Duck, or better yet, don't let him see you. All I want you to do is keep an eye on him and let me know where he is at all times."

Sam continues, "while you're doing that, I was going to go back to Newhall and see if I could locate Betty Langdon."

Lone Wolf turns and says, "You can let Kathy drive up to Newhall to find this lady. I'm sure Kathy would be glad to get out. How dangerous can that be for her?"

Sam's thinking, and then he says, "No, I don't want to take anychances and put her in a place that might be dangerous."

"Okay, if you say so. Well, I'll get started in West Hollywood. I'll check back with you later. You know if I'm going to put myself in harm's way all the time, maybe I <u>should</u> put in for a weapons permit."

"That does sound like a good idea. I can give you a letter telling thepolice that you work with me in cases where you might need to have one. You do know how to shoot, don't you? "

Lone Wolf looked at Sam with a (you got to be kidding me look) andcontinued, "I have four years in the Marines under my belt. I even have a marksman ribbon to impress the ladies.

I got that covered, and don't forget I'm also a badass biker." Then smiling back at Sam, he leaves.

Smiling back at Lone Wolf, he replies, "Great; I won't have to worry about you when you're out there trying to find the bad guys. Just keep an eye on him and let me always know where he is. Do you know anyone thatcan help you?"

"As I matter of fact I do, I'll swing by Maxx's Place and pick up abuddy of mine I can trust. You might be right on this one. This hitman could be a handful."

Then Sam speaks, "I'm going back inside and tell Kathy what's upand then I'll head up to Newhall. I'll have my car phone, so if anything comes up, call me."

When Sam enters the office, Kathy is busy at the computer. She is getting used to using it and getting familiar with the manual.

"Say, Kathy; I'm going to take a ride up to Newhall and see if I canspeak to Mrs. Langdon. I should be back in a couple of hours. Call me on my car phone if anything important comes up." Sam turns and heads out the door to his car.

He heads toward the freeway north and the intersection of 14 north. Getting off Lyons Ave exit, he heads down Lyons Ave to Miss Langdon's house. The closer he gets, he notices a lot of cars in front of the house.

They are Sheriff's cars, about three of them. They have that yellow crime tape around the front of the house. Sam pulls up and stops in front of the house and climbs out. He sees a tall man in a sheriff's uniform talking to someone.

He walks up to him and starts to speak, "Excuse me, sir, may I have a word with you?"

The man turns and addresses him, "Yes, can I help you."

Sam takes out his ID and says, "I'm a PI working on a case that concerns Miss Betty Langdon. I spoke to the man that lives in this house a couple of hours ago. He is her brother. Is everything okay?"

The man looked at him for a minute then said, "I'm Sheriff Jack Terrana, and I'm in charge here. We have not been able to locate Miss Langdon. Earlier today, Betty's brother was found shot to death inside the house."

"I'm sorry to hear that." Sam continues, "I just spoke to him this morning. I'm trying to locate his sister. She is a person of interest in a murder case I'm working on."

"I see well there is nothing I can tell you now. If you leave your cardwith the officer over there," – pointing to the gentleman over by the car – "I'll have him contact you as soon as we find out something, sir."

"Thank you, Sheriff, for your time; I'll be in touch." Sam turns andheads over to the officer and gives him his card and gets back into his car.

After leaving his card with the officer, Sam drives back to the office. He thinks the body count has started. When He arrives back at his office, he still hasn't figured out his next move. He figures he would wait and see what Lone Wolf has come up with and then talk to Kathy.

85

SEVEN

Sam didn't have to wait long as soon as he opened the door to his office, he saw Lone Wolf and Kathy standing there talking.

Sam spoke first, "My two favorite people are here good."

Kathy turned to the door and said, "Oh, Sam hi, I'm glad you're here. Lone Wolf just arrived and was telling me about his trip to West Hollywood."

Lone Wolf chimes in, "Yes, I was telling Kathy that the traffic on theHollywood Freeway was terrible, especially this time of the day." Sam walksover to his desk and sits down.

"What's the news?"

"Well, I took Mike my bud from the bar, and we both went to find Mr. Rampulla. We found his apartment, but nobody was there, so I told Mike to watch his apartment and call me when Mr. Rampulla makes an appearance."

Sam speaks, "Good, well, I have some bad news. Remember me telling you that Ms. Langdon had a brother, and she was staying with him,well when I got to his house today for the second time up in Newhall the sheriff was there. It seems that Ms. Langdon's brother had been murderedshortly after I left the first time this morning, and Ms. Langdon wasn't there. I'm not sure if she came home and found her brother dead and ran again or if she walked in, and Mr. Rampulla had just finished the deed andgrabbed her and took her and left. I spoke to the sheriff, and they told methey would let me know if anything comes up. In the meantime, I suggestyou stay with Mike and let me know the minute that Mr. Rampulla shows up."

Lone Wolf speaks, "Sounds like a plan I'll get a bite to eat and head back down to his apartment.'

Kathy speaks next, "Well, I can keep checking on the computer aboutMr. Rampulla and see if I can find anything that would be useful to the case. So far, I know his full name is Frank Rampulla, and he worked for theNew Jersey mafia up until nineteen-sixty, and then he left and went back to Lodi. He started with them back in nineteen-fifty as a bodyguard and money collector. They wanted him to check the Movie industry out here. Let's see, round nine-teen fifty-nine, that's when it started.
He came out here and started asking around the studios. After he had that incident withMr. Strand in nineteen-fifty-nine, he graduated up to their hitman. That's about all I should say now. They haven't been able to connect him to the Strand murder; that's where Ms. Langdon comes in."

Sam speaks, "Good work Kathy; now I'll get a letter off to a friend in New York, and he has a few connections to the 'Families' in the New York, New Jersey areas. Maybe he can tell us something." Sam goes to his desk and starts to write a letter to his friend.

Sam was into the letter for about an hour when he finally looked upand saw the time. He finishes the letter and addresses it and puts a stamp on it. He takes it out to Kathy's desk and drops it in her outbox then speaks, "Kathy, it's late do you want to go get a bite to eat?"

Kathy looks up and says, "No, I feel a little guilty about leaving myfather by himself all this week what with working here at the office every day and then staying at your place at night. I think I'll head home tonight and take dad out to dinner for a little payback."

Sam is a little disappointed he likes spending the time with Kathy, but he understands what she is feeling.

He speaks, "Okay, Kathy, that sounds good. I'll see you in the morning then." He turns and leaves, he crosses the garage and into the house just in time to hear the front doorbell. He heads to the door and opens it. What he sees surprises the hell out of him. It was an older woman with a much younger woman, a girl of about sixteen or seventeen.

He stared for a moment, not believing what he sees. Then he says, "You have got to be Ms. Langdon," looking at the girl he continues, "And you must be Marilyn. Won't you both please come in?"

The older woman is busy looking at the business card she got from her brother, and then she looks at Sam and says, "Are you Sam Ryan, the detective?"

"Yes, I am; I'm glad to have finally met you. We have a lot to talk over." he follows as Ms. Langdon and her daughter walk ahead into the living room. They both sit on the couch. Sam addresses them, "Why don't I get you two, something to drink. What would you like to have?"

Ms. Langdon speaks for both and says, "A couple of glasses of iced tea would do nicely thank you it's pretty hot out their today."

"Okay." Sam turns and goes into the kitchen to get the tea. A few minutes later, he re-enters the living room with the drinks and places them on the coffee table with coasters. Sam likes his coffee table too much to get glass rings on it. He sits opposite them, and all is quiet for the moment.

Ms. Langdon speaks first, "I have your business card I took from my brother. He was holding it in his hand when I found him." Her eyes were watering, and she was trying to be firm about it. The daughter was doing better. She had a sad face but did not look like she was going to fall apart any minute like her mother.

"I'm so sorry for your lost." Sam tries to console her. Sam continues, "I went up to Newhall earlier today and spoke with your brother. I told him to give you that card, and you could call me if you needed to. I went back a second time, and that's when I saw the police out front. I spoke to a Sheriff Terrana. I didn't go inside. Sheriff Terrana told me your brother had been murdered, and that's all he could tell me now. He did sayhe would get in touch with me if he heard anything new."

"Yes, and I apologize for not calling. It's just that everything happened so fast, and the next thing I knew, I was running and ended up here."

"Tell me, Ms. Langdon, when was the last time you saw your brother?"

"Please, Mr. Ryan call me Betty, and this is Marilyn"–she pointed to her daughter and continued- "I saw him this morning early about an hour after you left. My brother told me about you being there and asking about me. I went into the bathroom to freshen up, and I heard a gunshot. I waiteda minute or so, hoping he wouldn't come into the bathroom. I didn't know what to do. When I ran out to the living room, the person that shot him was gone, and my brother was lying on the floor dead. I saw the card in his hand and took it and left and went to pick up Marilyn and we both came here to see you."

"Did he say anything about what I wanted?

"No, he was already dead. Before I went into the bathroom, he did tell me it was important I give you a call. What is all this about, and why was my brother killed?" At that moment, her daughter Marilyn grabbed her hand and held it to console her.

"I'm going to start at the beginning." Looking at Marilyn and Betty, he starts with, "Is it alright to talk in front of your daughter?"

Ms. Langdon speaks, "yes, it is alright, over the years, I've told her everything, including about her father and the murder of Donald Strand and why I ran in the beginning."

"Okay, then I'll start with why I'm looking for you. About a week or so ago, a man came into my office explaining that he was Mr. Walters, and he was looking for his wife." Ms. Langdon looked a little surprised when I said this. I continued. "He told me you had run away back in nineteen-fifty-nine just after you filmed 'Some Like It Hot' and he was trying to findyou. He told me he had been searching all these years to try and find you with no luck."

Ms. Langdon looked a little uncomfortable as I talked about it, but she interjected with, "I… I had an indiscretion back then, and I'm not proud of it. Unfortunately, it ended up in a murder, and I witnessed it and was tooscared to stick around. The gentleman that made the killing I had never metbefore, and I was afraid that he would kill me if he knew I was there, so I went out the back and had been running ever since."

Sam said, "All that is understandable, but so much time had passed I don't understand why you didn't come forward before this?

"I was afraid that if I went to the police about it, the man would find me and kill me, and I was pregnant with Marilyn at the time and had to think of her too and what would happen to her if I turned myself in. I didn'tgo back to my husband because I thought I would be putting him in harm's way too. After Marilyn was born, I moved up to Newhall lived with a friend of mine. After she died, I moved down to Sherman Oaks. I'm living with a couple of friends of mine. Their names are David and Coleen Abraham. I know what I did was wrong, but now I'm here to get it right. Why were you looking for me? I had heard a couple of years ago from an old business associate that my husband was extremely sick and died if that is true, then who was the gentlemen that claimed to be my husband, and what did he want?"

Now Sam looks a little worried, "That's the twist in this whole thing. I took the client's information down and told him I would look foryou, and if I found out anything, I would let him know, and he left. A couple of days later, I had another visitor; a Mr. Hawkins was from the Allied Insurance Company. He told me he was looking for Mr. Walter's <u>widow</u>."

I could see the surprised look on both their faces and tried to explain it to them as well as I could. Sam continues, "It seems that your husband died a couple of years ago of a heart attack. The Insurance company was looking for you because your husband had left you a Life Insurance policy in case you came to your senses and returned after his death."

Ms. Langdon was confused and scared. "Did you ever find out whothe man is impersonating my husband was?"

"Well, that's where this twist comes in on the story. When the fake Mr. Walters came into my office, and we searched for you on the computer, it sent a red tag to the insurance company that someone else was also looking for you, and that's why Mr. Hawkins visited me. When he visited, he said he was looking for you because your husband had passed away twoyears ago and left you a life insurance policy worth Two Million Dollars, and Mr. Hawkins was looking for you to give you the check."

I thought Ms. Langdon and the daughter were going to faint. I continued, "I did a background on the fake Mr. Walters. Came up with thename Frank Rampulla, at the time he was working for the Mafia in New Jersey, he was a hitman, and Mr. Rampulla had come back to finish the job he started over thirty years ago.

Ms. Langdon, he came back to kill you andyour daughter. You were a witness to the murder of Donald Strand. Therefore, we have to go and find you a safe place to stay."

Ms. Langdon had a shocked looked on her face as did Marilyn. They both looked at each other, and Ms. Langdon spoke first, "We have to get out of here quickly."

Sam speaks, "Where did you go after you left your brother's place today?"

"As I said before when I came out of the bathroom, I must have justmissed the murderer. I went over to my brother and saw he was dead.

That's when I saw your card in his hand. I took it. When I turned it over, it had your address on the back. I went back to where I was staying and tried to put this whole thing together. It was all too confusing to me, so I decidedI would come to see you and hear what you had to say."

"I'm glad you did; now we can go from here. I have some personalfriends helping to find Mr. Rampulla in the meantime; we need to find a good hiding place for you and your daughter."

"Well, my daughter and I have been staying at a friend's place, as I said before over in Sherman Oaks. She and her husband have a room over the garage, which is good enough for both of us. Nobody that I know knows her except my daughter and me. When I first disappeared, I went to her place until I could figure things out."

Sam listened the whole time and then spoke. "That's all well and good, but now it's time to move forward. You don't have to worry about money for a while. I'll contact Mr. Hawkins and tell him I've found you, and we can work on getting you your money."

"Sounds great, my daughter and I could use it. We haven't had much money in the past. I took odd jobs to make ends meet. You know this whole thing started because I wanted to get into the movies and be a star. Ever since I was twelve, all I thought about back in Rapid City

South Dakota was becoming a star. I loved the whole idea of becoming famous. I moved out here as soon as I turned eighteen started having pictures made and going around to agents. It took me five long years of knocking on doors and getting propositioned, and doors slammed in my face before something finally happened. That's when I got this part in the movie with Marilyn Monroe Tony Curtis and Jack Lemon. I got so excited I couldn't wait until they started shooting. The first day I met Marilyn, she was so nice to me, I couldn't believe this was happening to me, then I met Charleshe was working props for the movie, he was so handsome, and I fell in lovewith him right away, it wasn't long after that that he proposed, and I said yes. I was on top of the world."

Sam was listening to her story; it was like a movie unfolding. Hewas all ears waiting to see what she said next. "What happened?"

"Well, Donald Strand was the AD on the movie." Betty turned to me and said, "That means Assistant Director." She smiled and continued, "Every time the Director had me do something, I would look to Mr. Strand for direction, and he would motion the direction I should move. I felt like he was my special teacher. He was always so friendly and nice. I learned a lot from him. After we wrapped up the movie, Donald asked me to go out and celebrate my first movie. I didn't see anything wrong with that.

Looking back now, I guess I shouldn't have encouraged him. I was so young and naïve I didn't realize at the time that he was just a dirty older man trying to take advantage of young girls' first time in Fantasy Land. By the time I put it all together, it was too late. I was pregnant by my husband, and Mr. Strand was murdered, and I was running."

Betty started to cry and looked at her daughter and said, "I'm sorry, honey, I didn't mean for all this to happen."

Her daughter just hugged her and said, "That's okay, mom; it's all over now, and we can leave this city and never look back." Then looking atme, said, "Isn't that right, Mr. Ryan?"

Sam is looking at them both and trying to sound encouraging even though he knew there was a lot to do before they could leave town, the least of which was to find Mr. Rampulla and put him away. He continued, "Yeah, that's right, but first we have to take care of a few things. At some point, you will have to speak to the police and give them a statement about the murder of Mr. Strand and who you saw do it and why you ran. Okay, forthe moment, you can stay at your friend's place in Sherman Oaks. My friend Lone Wolf and I are making plans to catch and arrest Mr. Rampulla and get him off your back. Then you'll be able to ID him for the Police,and that will take care of that. Don't tell <u>anyone</u> your address, and don't call anyone except me. It shouldn't take any more than a couple of days to clear this mess up, so stay patient. I'll drive you home tonight and watch you go in, so I'll know you are safe. Come on."

Betty and her daughter Marilyn followed Sam to the car, and he drove them home. By the time he got back to his place, it was late. It had been a long day. Sam was ready for a shower and some sleep. Tomorrow he could get Lone Wolf to follow him while he drives Betty's car back to her place in Sherman Oaks. He would explain everything to Kathy in the morning and bring Lone Wolf up to speed.

EIGHT

Morning came quickly, and as soon as Sam's feet hit the floor, they were moving. He got dressed and headed over to the office. It was about eight-thirty a.m. when he arrived. Naturally, Kathy was already there, andshe had made some coffee. Sam could smell it when he walked in. He loved that smell in the morning.

"Good morning Kathy ready for a full day?"

"Always Sam, say where is my morning Kiss?"

"I knew I forgot something." Sam walks over to Kathy and bendsover and kisses her on those sweet soft lips. "Hmmm, I missed those last night."

Kathy smiled and said, "Yeah, well, I'm sorry I had to go home."

"That's okay, I understand. Where did you take your dad for dinner last night?"

Kathy smiles, "Oh, we went to his favorite haunt, the Olive Garden. He loves that place. What about you, what did you eat without me around to cook for you." Kathy put that sexy smile on as she spoke.

"I didn't have any dinner. I had a special guest at my place when I got home last night."

Kathy stopped typing on the computer and folded her arms across her body with that 'oh really look' and said, "So tell me all about this mystery guest."

"Well, it was Ms. Langdon and her daughter Marilyn."

"You have got to be kidding okay so what did she have to say for herself?" She leaned forward in her chair; she was genuinely interested in Sam's story.

"She knows about her brother, and I told her who was after her, andhere is where you can contact her. Sam hands Kathy a piece of paper with all the information on it. Put this on the computer and throw the paper away, no burn it. We wouldn't want anyone to find it. Better yet shred it."

Sam gives Kathy the piece of paper with all the info on it. He walked over to his desk and sat behind it just as Lone Wolf walked through the door.

"Hello, everyone, and how are you guys doing this morning?" Lone wolf said with an enthusiastic tone.

Sam and Kathy both looked over at the door and said, together in unison, "fine."

Lone Wolf looked over at Sam and said, "Now that's what I callteamwork." He laughed.

Then Sam spoke, "C' mon over and sit we have a new development. I'll tell you all about it."

Lone Wolf walked over and sat next to Sam's desk. "Okay, shoot, I'm ready."

"First, I have to drive a car over to Sherman Oaks for a friend of mine. You can follow in my car and drive me back here." Sam proceeded to explain, "We found Ms. Langdon and her daughter, or I should say she found me last night. She paid me a visit at my home. Just as I arrived by way of my garage, there was a knock on my front door; it was her. She had the business card that I had given her brother. She said she found it in her brother's dead hand when she went to visit him the other day. She left in a hurry. She didn't want to have to answer any questions at least not right then."

"I don't blame her." Lone Wolf replied and continued, "I wouldn't be in any mood to talk to the police either."

"Yeah, well, for the time being, she is safe, but we have to find Mr. Rampulla and put him where he belongs before he finds them. Do we have any news as to his whereabouts?"

Lone Wolf speaks, "Well my friend Maxx said he doesn't stay at the same place too long, and he has the advantage of knowing where he will be next, and we don't know that makes it harder for us to keep track."

"See if we can find out about some of Mr. Rampulla's contacts. I mean he has been coming and going back east to here since the nineteen-fifties. He should know someone here. If we can get a line on some of his friends out here, we would stand a better chance of nailing him. In the meantime, I'm going to visit Sheriff Terrana up at Newhall.

Oh, Kathy, contact Mr. Hawkins and ask him how we can get part of that money that her husband left her, so she could buy some things that she needs to live on."

Kathy says, "Ok, what time can I expect you back?"

"I'll call you when I'm on my way back." Sam turns and heads out the door.

Looking at Sam, Lone Wolf says, "c' mon Bro' we should take that car to Sherman Oaks first, and I'll drop you back at the office, and then I'll go and check on Mr. Rampulla. Then you can go and do what you need to do."

Sometime later, Sam arrived at the Sheriff's office in Newhall. He parked the car outside and walked in. He saw a young officer sitting at her desk she looked up as he approached.

"Yes? May I help you?"

Sam spoke, "Yes, I would like to see Sheriff Terrana."

The officer smiled and said, "Yes, of course, could you please wait over there?" She pointed to a row of seats by the door.

Sam replied, "Yes, of course."

He walked over and sat at one of the seats. He looked around, and he noticed how empty it was. He thought to himself, 'I guess they don't have too much crime here in Newhall.' The office had about three desks, and two of them had somebody sitting at them. There was a fax machine in the corner of the room. Another woman was standing next to it. It looked like she was waiting for transmission. It was about that time that SheriffTerrana walked up to him and spoke.

"Well, it's nice to see you again." He held out his hand to shake.

Sam stood up and shook his hand, then said, "Yes, it's nice to see you again, Sheriff. I dropped by to see if you had any new info on our murder victim."

Terrana smiled and said, "<u>Our</u> Victim? I thought he was in my town."

Sam smiled back and said, "You're right technically, but he was involved in my murder investigation too, as a matter of fact, he still is."

Sheriff Terrana looked real serious for a moment, and then he started to break into a smile when he said, "Oh, okay C'mon in my office, and we can talk."

Terrana turned and headed toward his office with Sam following. They got into Terrana's office, and Terrana sat at his desk and told Sam to shut the door and relax.

Sam turned and shut the door and walked over to the chair and sat. He looked like a kid that was just let into the adult's office.

"Okay, I'm ready."

Terrana looked at him and spoke, "Well, to begin with, this is an ongoing investigation, so anything you hear is confidential got it?"

Sam had a look on his face of a man that had heard it all before, so he smiled and said, "Yeah, Yeah, I know all that; just get to the good part."

"Okay then, we found some prints, and we ran them. We haven't got the results yet, but we are pretty sure our shooter was a pro."

"I think I can help you there." Sam continued, "We found out that the prints belonged to a Mr. Frank Rampulla. He is a hitman from New Jersey. Mr. Rampulla came back here to finish a job he started back in nineteen-fifty-nine."

The look on Sheriff Terrana's face showed that he was surprised and amazed that a hitman would come to Newhall. Nothing ever happened in Newhall.

Terrana spoke with a surprising sound in his voice, "Are you sure? I mean, how did you find out who it was before we got back the results from our people? Also, why would a hitman from New Jersey come out here to kill someone not involved in your case?"

Sam said, "Well, the only reason I can think of was that the man saw his face, and when he found out that the man didn't know anything, he had to kill him so that he couldn't ID him."

Sam tried to explain, "I think his target was the victim's sister. She is the one that saw him kill an assistant director back in nineteen-fifty-nine."

"Nineteen-fifty-nine, well, that sounds like a cold case."

"Yes, the assistant director that was working on a movie back then, I believe the name of the movie was 'Some Like It Hot.' The prop man for that flick had a wife who was one of the members of the all-girl band in the picture. She was having an affair with the AD at the time a Mr. Strand. She was in the bathroom and saw the whole thing. Mr. Rampulla had been looking for her for the last twenty years. He found out after the fact that she witnessed the entire thing from the bathroom, so he had to find her and fix it so that she couldn't say anything."

"How did he find that out?"

Sam looked a little puzzled and said, "That we haven't got a handle on yet as far as finding out who the hitman was before you, my secretary's father is a retired policeman from the Burbank police force, and he did us afavor. The Burbank police contacted your department and asked for a copy of the prints your people found at the scene, and they would send you a copy of what they found. I'm sure if you check with your people, you will find you received a copy of the results this morning."

Terrana looked angry at first; then, after he thought about it for a minute, a small smile came on his face. "That's what I call cooperation between departments."

Terrana took a drink out of his coffee cup; it was a little cold. He made a face and moved the mug to the other side of the desk and spoke, "Okay, let's assume you're correct on what you've told me so far. Where do we go from here?"

Sam looked at him with a smile as if to say, 'I have a plan,' then spoke, "Well, I have a couple of my people on it. We know that Mr. Rampulla has lived out in Hollywood for a while now. Only he is a little paranoid about being found out, so he moves around, and that makes him hard to pin down. Mr. Rampulla doesn't live in the same place for awfully long. We also know he must have friends here, so he can't stay hidden. We are trying to locate anybody that knows or has been in contact with him."

"Good." Terrana said, "What can I do to help?"

Sam smiled again happy that the sheriff was on the same page as he then continued, "You work the murder from this side, and if I find anything out, I'll contact you, and you can go from there in the meantime you can follow up on your leads in the brother's murder. Who knows, maybe we both might get lucky." Terrana stood up with a smiled and extended his hand for an okay shake. Sam stood and returned the shake as he turned to leave.

Sam stopped and turned and said, "Oh, have you got one of <u>your</u> cards, so I can contact you if anything comes up? Here is mine." He handed Terrana the card and asked,

"Can I borrow your phone to call my secretary?"

"Yeah, sure, it's over there." While he is talking, he walks over to the desk in the corner and gets a card for Sam.

Sam walked over to the phone and called Kathy. He told her he was on his way back, and she could call it quits for the day and to go home. Then he hung up and went over to Terrana's desk they exchange cards andSam left.

It was close to four in the afternoon when Sam headed home. He got back to his house at about five p.m. Sam went and got a bite to eat. He hit the sack early, figuring on getting an early start in the morning.

NINE

Sam awoke about nine a.m. he finally slept all night without waking for something. He took a shower and headed over to the office.

What he saw when he walked into the office, he was not expecting. The place looked like a bomb hit it. The desktop computers were on the floor, and the file cabinet remained. The strange thing was that Kathy wasn't around. She usually arrived at 9 a.m. or earlier. Sam picked up the phone and called her dad to find out if Kathy overslept. He said she hadn't come home yesterday after work and he thought she was spending the night with him. Now Sam was getting worried. He told her dad he would get back to him as soon as he had something and not to worry. He hung up and called Lone Wolf. He told him what happened to the office and that Kathy was missing. Lone Wolf said he was leaving now and would be there within the hour.

Sam sat there for a moment to collect his thoughts and then started straightening the office. About an hour later, Lone Wolf walked in and started looking around.

Then Lone Wolf spoke, "What the hell happened here, and did you say that Kathy is missing?"

"Yes, I just spoke to her father this morning, and he said that she never came home yesterday when she got off work. I called her from Newhall yesterday at about four o'clock in the afternoon and told her I was on my way back, and she could go ahead and close and go home. I didn't see this mess until I walked into the office this morning."

Lone Wolf, with a concerned look on his face, looked at Sam and said, "Didn't you check the office when you got back? I mean, it's not like it's a couple of miles away. It's right next store."

Sam, with a mad look on his face, looked back at Lone Wolf and said, "I don't check the office all the time when I come home. I assume everything is smooth."

Lone wolf looked at Sam and said, "Okay, where do we go from here?"

"Not sure," Sam said. Just then the phone rang, and Sam answered it on the second ring, he pushed the speaker button and spoke, "Hello Sam's detective agency, who am I speaking to?"

"I think you know who this is, and yes, I do have your secretary, andI'll return her unharmed when you give me Ms. Langdon."

Sam had put the call on the speakerphone so that Lone Wolf could listen too. It was about then that Sam and Lone Wolf looked at each other for a moment, and Sam said, "How do we know you have her? Put her onthe phone."

The phone is quiet for a moment, and we hear Kathy's voice, "Hello Sam, I'm okay, just <u>do</u> as he says, or he <u>will</u> kill me." She sounded afraid.

Mister Rampulla got back on the phone and said, "Okay, now you know she is all right for now. When do I get Ms. Langdon?"

Sam spoke next, "Well, it's going to take some time to find Ms. Langdon. She's not nearby."

Mr. Rampulla speaks, "I'll call back in two days, and by the way, no police, you know what will happen if you do. I'll tell you where to bring her." Then he hung up.

Lone Wolf speaks first, "Well, we have two days to come up with something, now what?"

Sam spoke next, "This reminds me of an episode of 'McMillian and Wife.' Remember that series with Rock Hudson? He always won his cases without losing anyone. Well, do you know where we could get a double for Ms. Langdon?"

Lone Wolf's eyes opened wide as the light came on for him, then he smiled and finally spoke, "This is the town for doubles. But tell me again why we aren't using the real Ms. Langdon?"

Sam starts, "Well, if things go sideways, I don't want to lose our firstclient and Kathy too. So, tell me you have been here longer than I do you know anybody we can get to look like Ms. Langdon?"

Lone Wolf thinks for a moment then speaks, "It just so happens I know a woman that belongs to the movie-stunt union, and she is in pretty good shape. Let me make a few calls, and we'll see what happens."

"I don't want her in this much danger without offering her somethingfor her trouble, so tell her we could offer her five thousand for a two-hour job. I think the plan is a good one, so go ahead and make the call. I'll let you know about the rest of the plan as soon as we find someone.

Remember, we only have forty-eight hours. While you're doing that, I'll call Ms. Langdon and let her know where we are in this case and to warn her about how important it is for her to stay hidden for the next couple of days."

Sam starts to dial her number at the same time he pushes the button to the speaker. He wants to make sure that Ms. Langdon knows the plan. He hears the phone ring twice, and a woman answers.

He speaks first, "Hello, Ms. Langdon?"

The woman, on the other end, says, "No, who shall I say is calling?"

"Sam Ryan, a friend."

"Just a minute, I'll get her." After a moment, he hears a voice come on that sounds like Ms. Langdon.

"Hello, Sam, this is Betty, can I help you?"

Sam speaks, "Yes, Betty, I have some information for you concerning your case."

Ms. Langdon comes back with, "Yes, what do you want?"

"Well, Ms. Langdon, we have contacted Mr. Rampulla, and he wants me to bring you to a place of his choice. He is calling me back tomorrow and letting me know. The thing is there is too much danger in bringing you,so we are going to bring a woman that could pass for you. Since he has never seen you, I think we'll be safe in doing that. I have a friend that is contacting someone as we speak."

"Okay, if you think that would be a good idea, but I wouldn't want anything to happen to the woman that is playing me. Will she be safe?"

"Well, Betty, she'll be as safe as anyone in this situation."

"Ok, then I'm all for it."

Sam says, "Great, what I need you to do is stay in hiding with your daughter. I'm pretty sure he is unaware that you have a daughter. I don't want to put you or your daughter in harm's way if possible. I'll call you back after it's over, and everyone is safe."

Ms. Langdon speaks, "Okay, when will all this take place?"

Sam replies, "He is supposed to call me tomorrow at my office, and I imagine he'll want to meet us tomorrow afternoon sometime."

"Okay, I'll await your call back. Good luck."

Sam ends the phone call with "Fine." Then he hangs up. Sam leaves the office and heads over to the house to get a bite to eat while he awaits Lone Wolf's call. A couple of hours passed, and we find Sam sitting in his recliner opposite the TV, but it isn't on. He is deep in thought and wonders if Kathy is okay. His thoughts go back to when they met. It was during the first case he was on when he came out to go to his Uncle's reading of the will. It wasn't long after I had arrived, and Kathy had come over to ask me some questions. I had just gotten back from San Luis Obispo. She looked beautiful in the Navy Blue's she was wearing.

She worked at the Burbank P.D. as a rookie. I remember I was tired from the night before, and she was laughing at the bogus story I was feeding her,so I could get up the courage to ask her out. I was surprised when I finally did ask, and she said yes. I think I was in love with her from the very beginning. After the accident, I swore I would never put her in that kind of situation again, and now here I am with the same dilemma. Sam's memories were interrupted by the ringing of his phone. He jumped up and answered it.

"Hello, this is Sam." There was a pause while he listened to the person on the other end. Then he continues, "Ah yes, Lone Wolf, how did your search go." Again, he waited and then continued, "Great, I'll see you when you get here." He hangs up the phone and goes into the kitchen to getsomething to drink. Half an hour later and the doorbell rings. It is Lone Wolf. He has two women with him. He let them in, and they went into the living room. Sam looked at the two women and said, "Okay, I think an intro is in order here."

Lone Wolf smiled with that proud smile he does when he is pleased with himself and said, "This attractive woman to my right is Lola Black. She is a member of the Los Angeles chapter of the Stunt woman's union."

Sam shakes her hand and says, "Hello, miss Black; I'm pleased to meet you."

The brunette holds out her hand and shakes Sam's hand saying, "It's nice to meet you too." Sam knew right away; she had to have been working out. She had a strong grip.

Lone Wolf then introduced the other woman by looking at her and saying to Sam, "And this lovely woman is Carol Kasparian, and she works for the studios as a make-up artist. I thought we might need her to help Lola look older and closer to Ms. Langdon's age."

Sam shook her hand and said, "Good idea Lone Wolf I hadn't thought about that. She will come in handy. Now I told Lone Wolf I would offer five thousand for the job. I didn't know he would bring two of you, so I guess the fee will be five thousand for each of you."

He looked at Lola Black and said, "Well, did Lone Wolf fill you in on what we need for this job."

Lola looked at Sam and then said, "Yes, he said I was to play an older woman, and it's going to be risky."

Sam smiled and said, "You might say that. The man you're going to meet wants to kill you, but we won't let that happen."

"I hope not; I want to be in a lot more movies when this gig ends."

Sam continued, "Well, this should be a quick snatch and grab. We don't know exactly where it's going to be yet. We will find out tomorrow. I can't express too much, how dangerous this will be, the man is a hitman for the Mob, so if you want to back out now is the time. I'll understand if you don't want to do this."

The two women look at each other and nod; then Lola looked at Sam and spoke, "When do we begin?"

"Okay then, I have two bedrooms upstairs you can stay here for the night, and in the morning, Carol will fix you up, and we will wait for the call. Now the man has never met the woman he is supposed to kill, but he has kidnapped my secretary, and he is willing to exchange her for you and killing you who he thinks is Ms. Langdon. Does that make sense?"

Lola speaks, "I got all that, but what about me, what do you want me to do?"

"Well, we will probably be facing each other, and I'll suggest you walk toward her the same time she walks toward you. When she gets in front of you, grab her and take her to the ground, we'll do the rest."

"Sounds good to me," Lone Wolf replied.

Sam answered back, "Yes, in theory, it should work."

Sam looked at Carol and spoke, "I have a picture of Ms. Langdon; she gave it to me to put in my file. You can use it to make Lola resemble

Ms. Langdon when you do the hair and make-up on Lola so that she will look more like Ms. Langdon–at least from a distance."

Carol smiled and said, "That picture will help a lot when I start on her in the morning."

Sam continued, "In the meantime, you people must be tired, why don't we turn in it's going to be a busy day tomorrow."

Lone Wolf speaks, "Yeah, you guys better turn in I'll be back in the morning. See you." Lone Wolf turned and went out the door.

Sam and the girls are standing in the middle of the room, looking and feeling awkward. Finally, Sam said, "Let's go, ladies, I'll show where you will be sleeping tonight." He turned and walked up to the stairs the ladies followed. Sam was lying on the sofa had a hard time trying to sleep. He had a lot to think about, plus the fact he wasn't used to sleeping on the couch in his own house. He kept telling himself it's only for tonight.

TEN

Morning came quickly like a skier going down a very steep snowslope. He went into the kitchen and put on some coffee and made some toast for the ladies.

Sam set the table turned, and the ladies were standing there in front of him. Sam had to look twice at Lola. She had an eerie resemblance to Ms. Langdon. Lola was standing there with her hair in a bun slightly grey and wearing a faded blue dress down to just below her knees. She was wearing the kind of shoes you usually see on a middle-aged spinster that taught lower school in small-town America. It was the face that got his attention. Carol did a great job making Lola look like Ms. Langdon.

Sam turned to Carol and said, "Great job, Carol. Her daughter would think she was looking at her mother, at least from a distance. Come on in the kitchen, ladies, and have some breakfast. I can cook bacon and eggs, that's about the extent of my morning menu. Martha Stewart I'm not come to think of it. I couldn't even pass for the Brady Bunch's Mom."

The two ladies laughed as Carol said, "Sounds good to me. I don'tusually eat breakfast, mainly because the studio calls me about five in the morning, and I don't have time for it. But I make up for it with lunch."

Lola chimed in, "Then there is me, I'll have a couple of eggs and some bacon if you don't mind. You know what they say, 'Breakfast is the best meal of the day.' At least that's what they say."

Sam looked at Lola and replied, "You're right about it being the best meal of the day. I'll get started on those Bacon and Eggs." Sam turned and headed over to the stove. There was a knock on the front door. Sam turned and asked one of the ladies to answer it while he did the cooking.

Lola got up and walked over to the door and opened it. Standing in the doorway was Lone Wolf. Sam turned to look who was at the door.

Sam spoke first, "Well, now that everyone is here, we can get started on the plan I have."

Sam continued, "Okay, then the main ingredient for this plan is the location of which we don't have yet. Therefore, for the time being, we'll leave the location a mystery. Let's assume; for the time being, the location would be outside in the open, say away from people, and secluded. For the sake of this scenario, we'll say it's an open field with trees on both sides of the field. Now I will be at one end of the field with Lola, or rather I and Ms. Langdon, while at the other end are Mr. Rampulla and my secretary Kathy. Now I'll tell Mr. Rampulla to let Kathy come to me at the same time I let Ms. Langdon come to him. Lone Wolf will be on either side of the field behind a tree at this point. He will be carrying a rifle."

Sam looks at Lone Wolf and says, "I'm taking your word about having a marksmanship ribbon from the service. We hope for everyone's sake, he doesn't have to shoot, but in case he does I know he will use it. We don't know exactly which side of the field Lone Wolf will be. It doesn't matter which side of the field Lone Wolf is on just, so he is safe and hidden behind a tree out of sight.

Lone Wolf speaks, "That's it? Vague, isn't it?"

Sam replied, "Well yeah, but that's because we don't know the location yet. I want you behind the tree with a rifle in case Mr. Rampulla makes a wrong move toward Kathy. In theory, it should work. Now, remember this whole plan is changeable, depending on where we meet. We should wait in my office for Mr. Rampulla's call. After the ladies eat, we better move this to the office, so we'll be there when he calls."

When breakfast was finished, they all walked through the garage to Sam's office. It was a couple of hours later when the phone rang. Sam turned the speaker on and gestured to everyone in the room with a shh sign then continued, "Hello, Sam Ryan's Detective Agency this Sam Ryan, can I help you?"

A voice on the phone replies, "Mr. Ryan, this is Mr. Rampulla. I'mready to tell you where we are going to meet."

Sam speaks, "Let me talk to Kathy. I want to make sure she is alright."

There's a pause, then we hear, "Hello, Sam, this is Kathy, please be careful."

The voice is interrupted, Mr. Rampulla continues, "Okay, now you know she is okay. Now listen very carefully. Do you know the William S. Hart Museum in Newhall?"

Lone Wolf gives Sam the yes nod, and Sam continued, "I'll find it no problem."

Rampulla continued, "Alright, then bring Ms. Langdon with you to the back of the bunkhouse. There are three levels on the property with threebuildings on each level. The bunkhouse will be the first building. Don't get lost and be there at six p.m. tonight, no cops."

Sam replied, "I'll be there. You make sure that Kathy stays well, or you will have me to deal with, and trust me, you don't want that."

Rampulla says, "Yea sure, you just make sure you're alone except for Ms. Langdon." Mr. Rampulla hangs up.

Lone Wolf speaks first, "I know exactly where the museum is, I've been there sometimes. I follow the old west stars as a hobby."

Sam speaks, "Good then you be there at five p.m. I'll let you pick your hiding place to keep an eye on Kathy, make sure it has a good vantage point."

Lone Wolf continued, "Got it."

Sam keeps talking, "Lola, you stick to me like glue until I give you the signal to start walking."

"That's Right!" Sam could see that Lola was worried, so he said, "Say Lola don't worry about anything. Everything is going to work out fine. When this is over, you're going to be fine. Just think you will have astory tell all of your stunt buddies."

Lone Wolf piped in with a little antidote, "Say, Sam, did you knowthat John Wayne was twenty-two when the real Wyatt Earp died? Of course, at that time, Mr. Wayne's name was Marion Morrison. They changed his name later. The director John Ford discovered him on the set of one of the westerns he was working on at the time as a prop man. Theysay that John Wayne didn't care for Wyatt Earp, and that was because John Ford had a run-in with Mr. Earp about a script concerning his life story.

Ford didn't want to pay him for it, and Mr. Earp was upset and never got over the insult. Ford didn't like him after that, and Wayne went along with it. At least that's the way the story went."

Sam smiled and said, "I knew I kept you around for more than just ahelper. You're like a walking book of Hollywood history."

They all decided to sit and wait until it was time to go. After an houror so, Sam walked over to his desk to make last-minute plans. It was now four o'clock, which meant they had about two hours to get prepared for the big meeting. Lone Wolf and the ladies were busy getting the details together. By four-thirty p.m., they were ready. Sam was at the desk, looking at a map of the William S. Hart Museum property. Lone Wolf walked over to where Sam was sitting at his desk.

Lone Wolf speaks first, "What are you looking for?"

Sam replied, "I'm looking at this map I picked up at a tourist store when I first arrived here. I figured I would get there sometimes between cases. Anyway, I'm glad I did, anyway I want to get familiar with the area." Pointing to the Bunk House, he showed Lone Wolf the area and continued, "We don't know where Mr. Rampulla and Kathy are going to be. Where do you think the best place for you to hide?"

Lone Wolf looked at the map for a minute then pointed and spoke, "Right here is where I think it would be the best place for me hide."

Sam speaks, "Yeah, that looks like the perfect place." Then he looksat Lone Wolf and continues, "I'll look for you to give me a look when I'm in place. Be careful I don't want to have to write up any more paperwork than I must. Besides, it's hard to find a good partner, and I don't want to have to replace you."

Lone Wolf smiles and speaks, "Nice of you to care so much about me." Starring at Sam with a sarcastic smile and continues, "Well, I'm heading out now. I'll be there by the time you get there. Lone Wolf turned and left.

About an hour later, the rest of the crew headed out. They arrived atthe Museum parking lot. Sam knew that Lone Wolf was already at the place they discussed; he saw Lone Wolf's car parked in the parking lot for tourists. He hoped he picked a good position and was in place and ready.

Sam went to his car door, opened it, and said, "Okay, Ms. Langdon, kindly step out here and follow me to the place."

Lola looked at Sam and said, "Right, Mr. Ryan, I'm in your hands." She smiled and continued, "Please be gentle. Remember, I'm an old woman." Sam and Lola laughed together.

Sam spoke, "Okay, now, just be alittle more serious."

They both started to head over to the position Sam previously picked on the map. They had just arrived at the place, and Sam looked around. It was at that time Sam heard a familiar voice. He turned into the direction that the sound came. About forty yards straight ahead, he saw two figures. It was early evening, and the sun was starting to set. Off to his left about twenty yards away through the corner of his eye, he could see a figure. He hoped it was Lone Wolf, and then he saw Lone Wolf raise his hand discreetly. Sam felt better, knowing where he was. Sam forgot about starting with the sun at his back. But that gave him an advantage. That meant that Mr. Rampulla would have the sun in his eyes. That was police 101. Sam was mad at himself for not thinking of that small detail, but luck always comes into play in this kind of situation.

Mr. Rampulla spoke first, "Okay, Mr. Ryan; this is the way it's going to go down. Send Ms. Langdon to me first; then, I'll release your secretary."

Sam replies, "No, we'll start them both off at the same time on the count of three. One, Two, Three, and then go."

Mr. Rampulla replies, "Okay, but if you try anything funny, I'll shoot her right in the back of the head. Are we clear?"

Sam replies, "Yes." Then he says something out of the side of his mouth to Lola. "All right, are you ready? Remember, you know what you have to do."

Lola speaks, "Right, Sam, I got this no problem." Sam looked back at Mr. Rampulla and said, "Ready?"

Mr. Rampulla replies, "Okay, I'll start counting." With that, Samhears Mr. Rampulla start to count, and at the same time, he let's go of Kathy, and she starts to walk.

"One, Two, Three."

Lola and Kathy start moving toward each other. Sam sees Lone Wolf hiding behind the tree. From the angle that Mr. Rampulla was standing, Sam could tell that he wouldn't be able to see Lone Wolf. At the same time, Lone Wolf would have a perfect shot if he had to shoot.

Now the two women were almost next to one another. Sam could feel the sweat coming down his forehead, and he flashed back to a year agowhen Kathy was in danger. It was Déjà vu. He could feel his gun hand start to shake. His hand would always begin to shake very little, but it did shake at a time like this.

So, the scene was set. The women were heading toward each other; Lone Wolf was behind a tree with his trusty rifle, and Sam was standing and waiting. It was like High Noon, where Gary Cooper is up against the bad guys alone, and the bad guys were closing in. Only I wasn't alone; I had help.

Then it happened, Lola dove at Kathy and took her to the ground and Lone Wolf took a shot at Mr. Rampulla. Mr. Rampulla was surprised by the shooting. He was watching Sam, and Mr. Rampulla knew the gunshot didn't come from him. Before he could react, the women left. Lone Wolf had missed with his shot. But at least it distracted Mr. Rampulla, and it gave Lola time to get Kathy to safety. Mr. Rampulla turned and took off before Sam could get a shot off. Lone Wolf chased him but lost him in the woods. Kathy is all in one piece but shaken a little.

Sam spoke first, "Kathy, are you okay? What about you, Lola, you were great, are you alright?"

Lola was wiping the dirt off her clothes and replied, "Sure, I'm fine, a piece of cake."

Then Kathy spoke, "I was scared to death, but I'm okay now."

Kathy is a little shaken. Sam put his arms around Kathy and squeezed so tight that Kathy made a sound of pain. "I'm sorry, Kathy, I'm just so grateful that you're okay."

Sam suggested that they go back to the office for a drink. They all got together in Sam's car and drove back to the office.

When they got back to the office, there was a note on his door. Sam read it out loud it said, **"This is not over yet, we'll meet again."**

Sam opened the door, and they all went in and sat down. Kathy walked over to the countertop and brought out some glasses and a bottle of Scotch. She poured a shot in each glass and passed them around.

Lone Wolf spoke, "Well looks like we took round one."

Sam replied, "You're right about it being round one." Then he looked at Kathy and said, "Look, Kathy, I want you to go home and stay with your father. Mr. Rampulla doesn't know where you live. At least I don't think he does. Besides that, you will have your father there to watch you. Lone Wolf will take you on his way to take the ladies home."

Then looking at the ladies, he said, "Carol, Lola, I have a check foreach of you. Thanks for your help. We couldn't have done this without both of you."

"Mr. Ryan, speaking for myself, I had fun, and anytime you want something else done to call me Lola Black. Remember the name."

It was about that time that Carol had something to say, "That goes for me too."

Then Sam said, "well, to quote a famous cowboy from my youth. 'Happy Trails partners until we meet again.'" He walked over to Kathy, took her in his arms and kissed her, and said, "Kathy baby, I don't want to put you in any more danger. Do me a big favor and stay away for a while, at least until this case is over. I don't want anything bad to happen to you. You will be safe with your father until we catch this man, then we'll be all right."

Kathy looked at Sam like she was going to disagree and then changed her mind and said, "Okay, Sam, it was a little too much excitement for me. I'll wait for your call." Sam thought about what the doctor said about and how too much stress wasn't right for her.

"Yeah, great idea Kathy" Then he looked at Lone Wolf and said, "Lone Wolf, you make sure she gets home okay, then take the ladies back and come back here. Okay?"

Lone Wolf replied, "No problem, Sam. I'll see you in a couple of hours." He turned and headed toward the door the women followed. Sam watched the door shut behind them and went to the counter and poured a tall drink and sat at his desk. He thought to himself, 'I have to call Ms. Langdon and tell her everything worked out okay, and he would call back as soon as he decided his next move.' He sat there thinking about Kathy and wondering how this was going to turn out, but he was relieved that Kathy was safe.

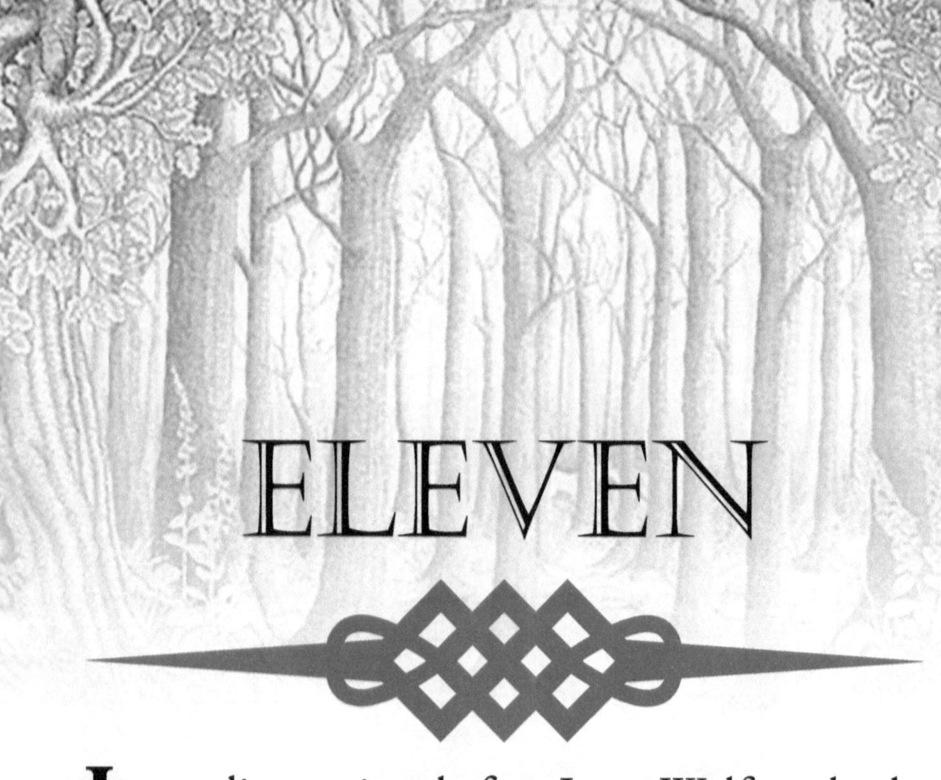

ELEVEN

It was dinner time before Lone Wolf got back. Lone Wolf walked in, and Sam said, "Did the ladies get home safe? How was Kathy? It had been a rough two days for her."

Lone Wolf replied, "Kathy looked very tired. She will probably sleep for a couple of days. Mr. Kelly (her dad) said he would watch her. When I took the ladies home, all they could talk about was you and the job they just finished. They both said that they felt so good after helping somebody. It was different than doing a stunt in the movies. Someone could get hurt. What we did today was real life, and it was gratifying. Theyalso said anytime you need someone to help with a case, feel free to call them."

Sam spoke, "That's nice. They were a great help, couldn't have done it without their help. Let's go out for some dinner, how about a good juicy steak?"

Lone Wolf speaks, "Sounds good to me; let's go to the 'Outback.' They have great steaks."

Sam was up and out of the chair before you could say 'hmmm good.' When they got to the restaurant and sat down in a booth, the waitress came over, and they ordered some drinks first, then the waitress left. Lone Wolf spoke first, "Okay, Sam; we have to get this guy before he gets us, so what's next."

Sam spoke, "Well, first thing in the morning, I'm putting a call into a temp agency to get somebody to take Kathy's place for a while. I want her out of danger for a while, and she could use the rest. Then I'm going to call my friend in New York that has some connections to the 'families' in Jerseyand Brooklyn and find out how Mr. Rampulla stands with the families.

Maybe I can get them to call off the hit on Mrs. Langdon. I'll let you knowin the morning. In the meantime, have your buddy keep an eye on his placein case he comes back there."

The waitress came with the drinks, and they ordered a couple of steaks. When they finished eating, they drove back to the office. Lone Wolf in his car and told Sam he would see him in the morning and drove off.

Sam closed the office and went through the garage to the main house. He opened the door, and before he could turn on the lights, someone hit him, and he went down like Shane (the character in the movie of the same name) in the bar when he got hit from behind by a chair. Sam wasn't down for the count. He got up in time to block another attempt to knock him down.

Now it was his turn. He started with a right jab and followed it up with an uppercut. The man went flying across the room and ended up on the floor. By the time he got up, Sam was on him like cat litter on a cat's paw. Sam hit him two more times before Mr. Rampulla went down again. He was like a ball bouncing off the floor. Mr. Rampulla turned and hit Sam a hard one to the face, and Sam went down for the count. A few minutes later, when he came to, Mr. Rampulla was gone. He turned the lights on to see the damage to the place. There was a note on the kitchen table; it read, 'Turn over Mrs. Langdon, or you will be sorry. Next time I won't miss.'

He started straightening up the place. It was about that time the doorbell rang. When Sam answered it, it was the police. Sam let them in, and he walked over to the couch in the living, and the uniform officer followed him. The police detective told the patrolman to read him his rights. Then he turned to Sam and said, "You want to tell me what happened here?"

Sam replied, "First, I'd like to know who called you because I certainly didn't have time." Sam was upset with the way the police were treating him, he continued, "Well, officer, it was just a simple case of breaking in. If you check with the Newhall police, a Detective Terrana, you may find out that the same man Mr. Rampulla was also involved with murder up there. Unfortunately, he got away."

The Detective replied, "Well, Mr. Ryan, we got a call from the neighbor across the street a Ms. Rottingham. We're not going to take you in, but in the morning, come on down to the station house and write out a report; oh yes, don't leave town." Then he smiled as he stopped writing and put the pad in his pocket and headed for the door and left.

Sam sat there with a smile on his face. Trying to think how many times he saw or heard that statement. Sam turned and went upstairs to get some well-needed sleep. Sam was thinking he was going to have to replacesome of the broken things in tonight's little grudge match. He would tell Lone Wolf about this in the morning.

The next morning Sam went down to the station to fill out the report. He wanted to stay on the right side of the law in case he needed them for help sometimes. When Sam got back to the office, the first thingSam did was call Lone Wolf to find out if our friend went home. Also, he wanted to know if Lone Wolf's friend Maxx saw anything. Sam asked Lone Wolf to come to the office, so Sam could tell him about the visitor he had last night. While he was waiting for Lone Wolf, he calls Kathy's father,Mr. Kelly, to find out how she was doing. He answered the phone with the usual hearty brogue.

"Hello, and who is it I will be speaking to?"

"It's me, Mr. Kelly. Sam, I was calling to find out how Kathy was doing."

Mr. Kelly speaks, "Well now first things first, I want to thank you for bringing her back safe and sound. Secondly, she is still upstairs sleeping. I figured I would let her sleep if she could. She needed it. Mr. Wolf explained everything, and I'll be sure to keep an eye on her and makes sure she stays here for a while."

"Good. I was hoping that Kathy could stay with you until all this mess was over and cleaned up. That way, we'll know that the bad guy is out of the way you know the one that threatens her."

Mr. Kelly was mad and said, "I want you to know one thing if ever I get my hands on the man, he won't need a doctor what he'll be needing is a coroner."

Sam smiled and said, "Well, I don't think you have to worry about that. Just make sure she stays home and away from this office for a while. Also, tell her I will be hiring a temp to take her place until this case is over, so she doesn't have to worry about the office work. We'll be fine."

With that, Sam hung up the phone. He called up the temp agency and asked for a gal Friday for a couple of weeks. They said they would send someone over today. It was then that Lone Wolf walked in.

Sam turned toward the door and acknowledged Lone Wolf and said, "I'll be withyou in a minute I have to call my friend in New York and find out if the Rampulla crime family in New Jersey knows what's going on out here." Sam picked up the phone and dialed his friend in New York. The phone rang twice before someone picked up and said hello. In the meantime, Lone Wolf went into the outer office and sat in the chair and waited for Sam to finish talking to his friend in New York.

Ten minutes had passed before Sam walked out of his office. He walked over to Lone Wolf and spoke. "Well, my friend in New York told me that the Rampulla crime family knows everything that's going on out here. He also told me that they are not happy with the results of Mr. Rampulla's work out here. My friend told me that they were upset at the way he handled the first murder back in nineteen-fifty-nine. When they sent him out here this time, he was supposed to take care of Ms. Langdon so that it couldn't come back on them, but he ruined that job too. So, at this minute, my friend told me that they are sending out a second hitman out here to eliminate Mr. Rampulla and take care of Ms. Langdon and her daughter. You know what that means. We should put Ms. Langdon and her daughter in a safer place until this mess is over."

Lone Wolf speaks, "Did your friend say what the name was of thesecond hitman we are going to have to deal with?"

"He did. It was Colin McDermott."

Lone Wolf smiled and said, "Isn't that a strange name for an Italian hitman?"

"Yeah, that's what I said, and do you know what he told me?"

Lone Wolf smiled again and said, "This I got to hear."

"He said he was a very close friend of the family. He said that Colinhad married into the family. It doesn't make sense to me, but then again, it wouldn't be the first time. Anyway, when my temp comes in today, I'll have her run a background check on him and see if we can get a picture of him and maybe a little bit more about him that would help <u>us</u> find him before <u>he</u> finds us."

TWELVE

It was ten in the morning when the temporary secretary arrived at the office. I was relieved to find that the temp was not as attractive as Kathy. I didn't want Kathy to think anything that would cause any problems between us. Her name was Sherry Winston. She looked to be in her early to late thirties with brown hair, and she stood about five feet five. After talking to her for about ten minutes, I was happy about her computer skills. They were outstanding. Maybe I'll learn something about computers andsurprise Kathy when she comes back.

I told Sherry to do a background check on Colin McDermott; then, I went into my office to do some thinking about this case. I was puzzled as to why the family would send another hitman, surely Ms. Langdon wasn't that important to the family.

I was pleased to find out that Sherry was right. She handed me the printout for me to then said, "Mr. Ryan, I think you are going to be very informed when you read what I found out about Mr. Colin McDermott. It was a very interesting and dangerous sounding." She turned and left me to the reading.

After reading what Sherry had found out, I agreed with her description of interesting and dangerous. It seems that Colin McDermott grew up in Brooklyn with his parents. His mother died of Diabetes when he was sixteen, and his father owned a bar on the corner of Fifty-First Street and Fifth Avenue. It was called Jerry's bar after his father. When he was eighteen, he met a pretty girl in Coney Island. Her name was Harriet Rampulla. They eventually got engaged. He didn't find out that she was the daughter of the notorious Rampulla family in New Jersey until after they were married. After they got married, he worked for the family as the money collector. It didn't take long for him to work up to one of the Hitmen for the family. His first hit was an owner of an Italian Restaurant in Lodi, who was giving the family some problems. After that, he was in with the family. Now he was coming out here, for what I wasn't sure. I had to find out if it was to kill Ms. Langdon and her daughter or to eliminate Mr. Rampulla to tie up loose ends. Priority for me right now is to find a safe place for the Langdons. Sam leaves his desk and goes to the door and opens and speaks to Sherry from the doorway, "Sherry get Ms. Langdon on the phone and tell her I would like to come and see her today and get the address where she is staying in Sherman Oaks."

Sam turns and goes back into his office. After a few minutes, Sherry knocks on his door and opens it. She is waving a piece of paper in her hand. She speaks, "I got a hold of Ms. Langdon, and she said it would be fine for you to come over. Here is her address I wrote it down for you. I also put her phone number down in case you need it."

Sam gets up and takes the paper from Sherry. "Thanks, I'll be back in two hours. If a Mister Lone Wolf comes by, tell him where I am in casesomething comes up, and he needs to get a hold of me." While he is talking, he turns and goes out of the garage door and heads for his car. The Garage door opens, and Sam drives out and turns right, heading toward Sherman Oaks.

Sam pulls his car up in front of the address that Ms. Langdon gave him and looks at the house and thinking what a great place to live. He walks up to the front door and rings the door. When the door opens there inthe doorway stood a lovely blond. She had that Paige-boy look and about five and a half feet tall. She spoke first, "Hi, you must be Sam Ryan, my name is Coleen come on in."

"Thank you." I walked into the living room, and Ms. Langdon and her daughter Marilyn were sitting on the sofa. I sat on a chair next to her. "Good afternoon, folks."

Betty speaks first, "Hi Sam; I want you to meet my good friends Coleen and David Abraham. They live here."

Coleen extends her hand and shakes Sam's hand as she speaks. "Hello, Sam Betty has told me all about you."

Sam smiles and replies, "I hope it was all good."

David is the next person to speak, "We told her we only wanted to hear good things about you. We try to keep things positive in this house."

"I'll keep that in mind when I give my report. For now, I do have asuggestion for Betty."

Betty speaks, "What is that Sam?

Sam speaks reluctantly, "There have been more threats from Mr. Rampulla. His threats have implied he was not finished. Also, we have a development that has come to our attention. The Rampulla family in New Jersey is not happy with Mr. Rampulla's efforts and is sending another manto take over the job." Then he speaks directly to Betty and her daughter. "I think we need to move you to a safe house out of Los Angeles."

They all look at each other with puzzled looks on their faces.

Coleen starts to speak, and David interrupts. "Coleen and I have a cottage up at the Santa Barbara area that only her and I know about." Coleen was smiling and grabbed David's arm. Now she speaks, "Yes, I think what David is trying to say is that Betty and Marilyn can stay there until thingsget right."

Betty looks a little uneasy and speaks, "Coleen, Marilyn, and I appreciate your offer, but we can't impose on you like that."

"Don't be ridiculous. You're not imposing. We <u>want</u> you to use it,and that settles it."

Sam speaks, "That might work. We need to get you settled up there as soon as we can."

David jumps in, "Well I own a Cessna 172 it seats three passengers and the pilot. I could fly them up in the morning. It's only a forty-minute ride from here by plane."

Sam has a surprised look on his face, "You're a pilot?"

David smiles and answers with, "Yes, going on four years now. I have about five hundred hours. I'm studying for my Commercial license now." Then with a somewhat look of wonder on his face, he continues, "Don't know when I'm going to take the test though. If I'm lucky, I'll get it by the end of the year."

Sam getting a little excited about the idea of him being one of the passengers, says, "That sounds like a plan to me. I'd love to go with you if you don't mind." Then with a straight business look on his face, he continues, "That way, I could inspect the place and see if we need to add anything. Also, it would bring back memories of when I was flying in South Dakota. Back in the day."

Coleen speaks next, "Well, I don't think you will have to add anything. I mean, it's just a cottage. It has six rooms and a bath right on the shoreline. There are no other houses around, and it's about a mile from the main road."

Sam speaks, "Okay then, we'll meet here in the morning, say nine am. How does that sound?"

"That works for me." David continues talking, "The office will be closed tomorrow. I'll call Harry over at the hanger and tell him to get it ready for a morning flight."

Coleen gets her two cents in, "Well, I guess I'll stay home tomorrow, that way I can work on a few things I've got to do around the house."

Betty speaks up, "I don't know what to say. I appreciate you guys letting Marilyn and I stay there."

Marilyn speaks, "Mom, you <u>do</u> know I've never been in a plane, right?"

"Oh, honey, you'll love it. It's perfectly safe." Looking at David and Betty continues, "Right David?"

David smiles and says, "Oh, yes, it is. A plane trip is safer than a car rides these days, and you don't have any stoplights to stop for." They all laugh.

Sam pipes in, "Okay, then tomorrow it is. I'll meet you all here about eight-thirty in the morning. Right now, I have a few things I have to do before the trip in the morning, so I'll be going."

THIRTEEN

Sam woke up and looked at the clock. It showed five-thirty. He decides to get up and put some coffee on before he jumps into the shower. He goes to the front door and opens it to check the weather. When he looksup, he sees nothing but clear skies. That makes Sam happy he shuts the door and heads to the kitchen to put some coffee on and then goes in to take a shower.

About a half-hour later, Sam is sitting at the kitchen table having some toast and coffee while he thinks about the flight, he'll be taking in about two hours. It's been a while since Sam had gone up in a private plane, so he gets a little anxious thinking about it.

Yesterday when he came back from Coleen's house Lone Wolf was at the office along with Sherry. When he told Lone Wolf what he would be doing today, Lone Wolf just smiled and replied, "Well, I'll spend the day working on my bike."

Sam gave Sherry the day off and closed the office. Then he called Kathy and told her what his schedule was for today. She was glad he called and told her, that way she wouldn't worry. Sam got in his car and headed toward Coleen and David's house in Sherman Oaks.

Sam arrived in front of the house at eight-thirty am. Everybody was waiting outside for him. David walked up to Sam's car and started to speak.

"Glad to see you could make it." Smiling, he continued, "You can park over there. We're all going in my car."

Sam replied, "Great, I'll just park across the street." They all piled into David's SUV and headed toward Van Nuys Airport. When they arrived at Van Nuys, David parked the car next to hanger 121, and they all got out of the car and went inside the hanger. The hanger was big enough to hold three small planes, but now there were only two planes. One was probably rented. I noticed when we got out of the car, that a man was standing on the corner of the hanger watching. He looked out of place. Anyway, we continued into the hanger and loaded our luggage while David did a pre-flight check on the plane.

Sam sat in the front seat, and Betty and Marilyn sat in the back, and David just climbed into the pilot side. They didn't have to file a flight plan because they weren't going to be flying on instruments. So, he called the tower to get the runway number and permission to take off. Before you knew it, they were in the air and heading toward Santa Barbara. It was a beautiful day for flying. It reminded Sam of when he used to fly when he was in the Air

Force. Even though his primary job for the Air Force was working on computers, he was taking flying lessons on the side. It was a hobby. He used to fly solo around Mt. Rushmore. Great times. This flight turned out uneventful. They flew north along the coast all the way.

Nobody said much, and they were all busy looking at the beautiful view. The whole flight time was about forty minutes. David had called ahead for a rented car to meet them when they arrived. When they unloaded the luggage and loaded them into the car, they were off. The trip from the airport to the cottage was about fifteen minutes.

They arrived at the cabin a little afternoon. While Marilyn and Betty went inside, Sam decided to walk around the perimeter of the house and look for things he might have to change. He was surprised to find out hewouldn't have to change a thing, so he went inside. It was a delightful cottage, just like David had described it to them. Sam went over to talk to Betty, and Betty was talking to Marilyn. Sam started to speak, "Well, Betty, I just checked outside, and I think this place is going to be just right for you and Marilyn."

Sam looked at David and said, "The only thing I'm concerned with is if they have a surprise visit from our uninvited guest, is there a place for them to hide?"

David thinks for a minute then replies, "We have a locked attic, and when you get up there, you can pull the ladder up with you, and nobody can then climb up."

Sam replied, "That will work."

Betty turned around and started talking to Sam, "How long do you think we are going to have to stay here? I don't want to put Coleen and David out."

Just then, David came in from the kitchen and walked over to Betty and Sam and spoke, "Betty, I had the delivery man fill the refrigerator with all the food you will need for a month, so don't worry about putting us out. We won't be able to come here for a while so that you will have it all to yourself". I also had the cable man turn on the cable system so that you will have plenty of television."

Betty spoke, "David, I don't know what to say you and Coleen have been so good to us. How will I ever be able to thank you for all your help?"

David replied, "You and Marilyn are our dearest and closest friends, and we wouldn't have it any other way. So, don't even think for a minute that you should pay us back. Besides, it's only temporary, so enjoy it while you can when all this is over, and Sam here can catch the bad guys we can all continue our life's just like before."

Sam walks over to Betty and hands her his card then speaks, "Betty, if you need anything day or night, just call me at this number."

Betty smiles and says, "Sure, I got it. Okay, now that we got thatsettled, now what?"

Sam speaks first, "Well if David is ready, we can head back andleave you two to yourself."

David chimes in, "I'm always ready. I was trying to think if I forgot to tell you anything nope got everything." Sam and David walk toward the door and say their goodbye's and open the door and leave.

On the flight back, Sam is thinking about Kathy; they haven't seen each other in a while. He decides to call her when they get back and ask her if she would like to go to dinner tonight. They had a tailwind, so the flight was shorter than when they went— arriving at Van Nuys about four in the afternoon. Sam called Kathy rightaway. She was happy to hear from him.

"Sam, I'm so glad you called. When are you coming over?"

Sam smiles, "Well, honey, I thought maybe I could take you todinner tonight. If you're up for it."

"Are you kidding? I have been in this house a week without any company. Come on over, and I'll be ready when you get here. Where are we going to eat?"

Sam replies, ay place you want to go, you pick the place."

Kathy says, "Great; I know just the place."

"Really?" Sam says and then continues with, "Where is that?"

"I'll tell you when you get here."

Sam speaks, "I'll be over in about an hour. Bye, sweetie." Sam turns to David, who is smiling.

"Well, Sam looks like you are going to be busy tonight."

Sam, holding in a smile, says, "Yeah, it looks that way; let's go."

Sam and David turn and head toward the car. When they get back to Dave's house, it is almost five in the evening. Sam tells David he will call tomorrow and check on everything. He turns and heads to his car. He's thinking of Kathy.

FOURTEEN

When Sam got home it was about six-thirty he jumped in the showerand afterward got dressed. He called Kathy before he left to let her know he was on his way.

When he arrived at Kathy's house, she was ready and beautiful. While Sam is looking at her, he says, "The funny thing is when I see you again in person, you're more beautiful than the last time." He leaned overand gave her a long kiss. When they broke for some breath, Kathy spoke.

"That's what I love about, not seeing you for a while. You say the sweetest things. They both laughed, and Kathy continued, "C' mon we better go, or we will never make it to the restaurant."

They both turned and headed to the car. When they got to Chart House in the marina, it was almost eight in the evening. They were just in time for their reservations. They went inside. The waiter sat them by the window so that they could see the whole marina. It was beautiful at night you could see all the boats with their night lights on. You could always understand one lone boat heading out for a night ride, or maybe they were heading to Catalina. The waiter came, and they ordered. The waiter left, and Kathy spoke, "So Sam, how was your day?"

Sam answers, "It was great. I took a plane ride to Santa Barbara and settled Betty and her daughter Marilyn into a nice cottage on the ocean. Their friend Coleen and David Abraham owned it."

"That sounds nice."

"I'm satisfied that they will be safe for the time being, although there was one strange thing at the Van Nuys airport this morning when we were getting ready to leave."

Kathy looked curious and spoke, "What was that honey?"

"Well, a man was standing at the end of the hanger when we left to take off, he was wearing a hat and shades and a Long outer coat. He looked like Mr. Rampulla, but I might be mistaken."

"Honey, that could have been anyone. Maybe your wrong about who it was."

"Yeah, maybe, but I need to find out where he is. I'll check withLone Wolf in the morning."

Just then, the waiter brought them their drinks and took their order. After dinner, they took their regular walk around the marina. Samloves those walks at night with Kathy, and so did Kathy.

Sam speaks first, "I sure do miss these walks with you, and the time Ispent with you."

"I know, so do I." Kathy replied, then continued, "How is the case doing? Everything going okay at the office? How is the new girl doing?"

"Whoa! Honey, too many questions at once, let's see, how is the case? Well, it is going fine I have Betty and her daughter in a safe place for now, and Lone Wolf is trying to find the two men 'Rampulla and McDermott' that are trying to get to her. You know it's like a cat and mouse sort of thing. Let's see the second question, the office. Well, the office hasn't changed, still the same old place." Sam is not smiling. "The new girl, she's okay. I think she will work out okay until you get back. She isn't as good as you, but she has been around computers a little longer than you, so she knows computers."

Kathy looks at Sam with that sly look she knows he loves and asks, "Is she as pretty as me?"

Sam is now trying to hold back a smile as he speaks, "Well, let me see." He steps back and looks Kathy up and down and says, "Hmm, she is not as tall as you, and she is a little overweight, and she has short black hair. No, I'd say she doesn't compare to you at all. You are much prettier."

Kathy smiles and says, "You always know the right answers don't you, Sam? That's why I love you."

Sam speaks, "I have a great idea why don't you stay with me tonight,and I'll take you home in the morning."

They are standing very close and facing each other, and Kathy looks up at Sam and smiles, then answers, "I thought you would never ask."

Then they kissed a lengthy kiss. They turned and headed to the car holdinghands and staring at each other like two people in love. Sam pulls into the garage and both head into the house.

Inside, Kathy turns and hugs Sam and speaks, "I'm going to jump into the shower. I'll see you after that upstairs." Kathy goes upstairs, and Sam goes into the living room. He notices the light flashing on the phone, and it shows he has a message. He pushes the button to hear it; a voice comes on that he recognizes as Rampulla's.

"Sam, we're not through yet. We will meet again, and I will find out where you have hidden Betty and her daughter." The phone beeps end of messages, and Sam hangs up. He decides to call Long Wolf he figures he is at Maxx's this time of the night, so he called and asked to speak to Lone Wolf. He hears, "This is Lone Wolf."

Sam speaks, "I know I can recognize the voice. Listen, this is Sam. I just got back to my place with Kathy, and there was a message on my phone from Rampulla. Have you located him yet?"

"Well, I have a handle on where McDermott is, but Rampulla is into the wind."

Sam replies, "Well, I think I saw Rampulla at the airport hangar today when we took off for Santa Barbara. He wasn't there when we got back."

Lone Wolf replies, "What's next, Sam?"

"I don't know yet. Let me think about it. Can you come to the office tomorrow morning around nine? We can talk then, okay?"

"Sounds good to me, Sam. I'll see you then. Bye."

Sam says goodbye and hangs up. Then he hears a familiar voice from upstairs, "Sam, are you coming up?"

Sam replies, "On my way, Honey." Heading toward the stairs, he turns off the living room light and goes upstairs.

When he gets to the doorway to his bedroom, the lights are out. Hespeaks, "Kathy, are you in here?"

Kathy speaks in her unique sexy voice, "Sam, don't be silly, ofcourse, I'm here. Come on over and climb into the bed."

Sam replies, "Hmm, that sounds like a good plan." He walks over to his valet chair and undresses and climbs into bed. He puts his arm around Kathy and replies, "Why you have forgotten your jammies."

"Don't be silly, what do I need jammies for?" She put her hands on each side of his face and gives him a slow, soft kiss. He responds by kissing her back. Sam is thinking to himself, "Let the games begin." His hands start taking trips all over her body, the intimate places on her body that love to be visited. She loves it when he does that, and she starts kissing him harder and more profound.

And so, the night goes on as it should. Seeking all the pleasures theycan handle. When it's over, they fall into a deep sleep in each other's arms.

FIFTEEN

$\mathbf{M}$orning came quickly. The sun was showing through the window, and Kathy woke up first. She laid there and watched Sam sleeping. Kathy thought Sam always looked cute with his eyes closed his chest rising up and down with each breath. She leans over and gives him a soft kiss. Sam's eyes open, and he looks at Kathy.

Then he speaks, "Good morning, honey, I just had a wonderful dream, and now I discover it isn't a dream." He kisses her back then speaks again, "C' mon I've got to get you home. I'm expecting Lone Wolf at nine at the office."

Kathy looks at Sam and speaks, "Okay, but I'm doing it under protest." She kisses him again and throws the covers off and reaches for her nightgown on the chair. She gets up and goes into the bathroom.

Sam lies there for a minute, thinking of how lucky he is to have someone like Kathy. Then he gets up and starts to dress.

Sam drives Kathy home and heads back to his office. When he arrives at the garage, it is almost nine. Sam gets out of the car and goes into the office. Sherry was busy writing at her desk. She looked up and said, "Mr. Ryan, you had a call this morning. A Mister David Abraham wants you to call him back as soon as you can."

"Okay, put a call in to him, and I'll take it in my office." Sam turns and heads into his office and sits behind his desk as the phone rings. The phone rings, and Sam picks it up and says, "Hello David, how are you this morning?"

David speaks, "Good morning, Sam, look the reason I'm calling is I just received a call from a Mister Rampulla; he just warned me, Sam. I think he knows we're hiding, Betty."

Sam was hoping this would bring out Rampulla, but he didn't think it would be this fast. He speaks, "Don't worry, David, he is doing what I had hoped he would. The only thing is I didn't expect it this fast. All right, this what we are going to do. I'll make a call, and I'll have someone out to your place in about an hour. Stay close to home and take care of Coleen. My friend will take care of everything. I'll call you back in a little while."

Sam hangs up. Just then, Sherry buzzes him from her desk to tell him that Mr. Lone wolf is here. He replies, "Oh good, send him in. He's just in time." Lone Wolf opens the door and walks in and sits opposite him at the desk.

"Good morning Lone Wolf, how are things going? Have you located Rampulla yet?"

Lone Wolf replies with some concern, "No, not yet, but we have McDermott where we want him. We can pick him up at any time we want him."

Sam is happy about that and replies, "We'll keep him there. Now we have another problem. Rampulla made an appearance well, not an appearance, more like a phone call to the Abrahams. He doesn't know where we're keeping Betty and her daughter, but he did see us get into the plane at Van Nuys and knows we have her someplace near. More importantly, he knows that the Abrahams owned a plane and used it to hidethem. I need to ask you a favor."

Lone Wolf is smiling, replies, "Finally some actions, what do you want."

Sam speaks, "Well, I hope not too much action, but I need you to gettwo of your friends, one that can take care of themselves and wouldn't minddriving up to Santa Barbara and keep an eye on Betty and her daughter. I'llgive you the address, and I'll also make a call to Betty and let her know thatwe're sending somebody to keep an eye on her. Your other friend can hangout at

David and Coleen's house and keep an eye on them. I'll call and let them know that they are getting some help."

Lone Wolf speaks, "I have just the two guys in mind for the job."

Sam replies, "It's important that he can take care of anything that comes up. At least until I can figure out what we need to do."

"Oh, don't worry about that, the two guys I have in mind will do nicely. The one I'll send to Santa Barbara, we call him Truck he is about the biggest person and the best for this job. He is six feet eight and about two hundred and seventy pounds. He is the best at what he does. The other guy we call 'Snake' because you can't even figure out where he is going to be next. He can also take care of himself."

Sam replies, "We'll get him up there as soon as you can, and I'll call Betty and let her know he is on his way. I'll also call the Abrahams and let them know about Snake. Now on the

McDermott thing, I think we should send him back to the Rampulla family in New Jersey with a message.

Make sure he gets on the plane east today, and I'll give you the money for aone-way plane ticket. That should keep him out of our hair for a while."

Lone Wolf speaks, "What's the message you are going to give the Rampulla's?"

Sam thinking says, "We'll tell the family that we will take care of Rampulla quietly and keep the family out of it at the same time. That should satisfy the family."

Lone Wolf is smiling, "Yeah, that should do it."

Sam smiling "if I remember correctly back in my younger days in Brooklyn, families like that don't like the publicity of any kind, mainly bad. Yeah, that will keep the family off our backs until we can take care of Rampulla. Go ahead and make that call to 'Truck' and get the ball rolling at that end."

Lone Wolf turns and goes to the outer office to make that call. Sam stops Lone Wolf before he leaves and says, "You know Lone Wolf when this is all over, and everything is said and done I'm going to have to throw a party for you and the guys."

Lone Wolf is smiling, and heading for the desk says, "Sounds like a plan to me, Sam." as he continues to pick up the phone and dial Maxx's Place.

Sam sits at his desk for a while then decides he better go and check on David and Coleen. He walks out to the outer office to speak to Sherry, "Say, Sherry, I'm going to run over and check on the Abrahams if you need me. Their phone number is on the computer. Oh yeah, something else, do me a favor call Detective Terrana in Newhall and see if he has anything new on Betty's brother's murder."

Sherry replies, "No problem, Mr. Ryan."

Sam turns and heads for the garage and gets in the car to go to VanNuys. He arrives about noon and knocks on the door. The door opens, and Coleen is in the doorway smiling and speaks, "Mr. Ryan, glad you're here David wants to talk to you. He is just on his way to the office C'mon in."

Sam walks to the living room David is coming from the kitchen, a thermos, and a bag in his hand. Sam speaks, "David, looks like you have lunch already made, are you going to eat a little later at the office? Coleensays, you wanted to talk to me?"

David puts the bag and thermos down on the table and speaks, "Yes,Sam, sit down. I have a couple of things to tell you."

Sam sits at the dining room table and continues, "I'm assuming it isabout that phone call you got from Rampulla."

"Yes, it is, now I'm not usually scared by too many things, but this Rampulla person scares me." He sounded intimidating. "Have you any idea what he intends to do?"

Sam looking serious, begins to talk, "Let me start by saying he meanteverything he said. He is a hitman for one of the Mafia families in New

Jersey, so before he gets going, his main weapon of choice is fear. He'll try to get what he wants with fear first, and if that doesn't work, he'll go up the ante with a gun."

David speaks, "If you are trying to frighten me, it is working."

Sam speaks, "Slow down, David. It is not going to get that far. The Newhall police are looking for him regarding a murder in Newhall, and the Los Angeles police are looking for him for a cold case. So, he has more to do than work on you. I'm going to have a person outside your place twenty-four-seven watching the house. He is a good man. I recommend you stay at home for a couple of days until we clear this up. I don't think you need to worry. He's looking for Betty and her daughter, and what he wants from you is the where are the two of them. He won't get close enough even to ask you. Now if he calls you again, you tell him I visited you and told you we had moved them again and I wouldn't tell you where. That means he will have to come to me to find out and I'll wait for him.

Got it? You and Coleen will be safe here, stay close, and don't let anybody in the house except me and the police. I'll call you when the situation changes."

Sam turned and walked outside to the front of the house. Just as he got to the open-air, he saw a motorcycle pulling up in front of the house.

The gentleman that was riding the bike was a pretty portly guy. He was the regular biker with his leathers on with chains hanging all over. He parked the bike and walked up to me. He looked as though he had a few fights in his past. His nose is broken, and when he smiled, he had two teeth missing—one on each side of his mouth. Except for the missing teeth and the broken nose, he wasn't a bad looking guy. He held out his hand to shake, and Sam did the same. While they were shaking the biker said, "Hi, my name is Maxx, you must be Sam. Lone Wolf described you perfectly."

Sam replied, "Nice to meet you. I've heard some good things about you from Lone Wolf. Do you know why you're here?"

"I think so. Lone Wolf said you needed someone to keep an eye on ayoung couple and see to it they don't get in any trouble. Is this the place?"

Sam replied, "Yes, it is. Come on in; they are inside. I need you towatch them and to make sure no one disturbs them."

Sam hands him his business card and continues, "If anything happens, you can use this card to call me day or night. Did Lone Wolf tellyou what you could expect?"

Maxx smiles and replies, "Yeah, he said some guy might try to harmthem, and I'm supposed to discourage him from doing it. I'm looking forward to doing just that."

"Great, all right, then I'm going to leave now. Remember anytime day or night." Sam gets in the car and heads back toward the office.

When he gets back to the office, he notices that Lone Wolf's bike parked out front. He wasn't expecting Lone Wolf until much later. Something must have come up. He puts his car in the garage and heads toward his office.

When he walks in the office, he sees Lone Wolf standing over next to Sherry's desk. He didn't look thrilled.

He speaks, "Hello, Sam, I've got some bad news for you."

Sam didn't know if he was ready to hear it or not, but he knew he was going to anyway. He says, "Why do I have the feeling I'm not going to like it."

Lone Wolf replies, "You right, we lost McDermott. We didn't gethim on the plane as planned."

Sam speaks, "Great, what else can go wrong."

Lone Wolf replies, "it's not as bad as it sounds. We have been keeping track of him, and we know all the places he has been hanging out.So, unless he has a place we don't know of, we'll pick up his tracks again.I've got everybody watching for him. He can't hide for long."

Sam speaks, "Okay, so remind me again who we have watching Betty and her daughter in Santa Barbara?"

Lone Wolf replies, "I have Truck and Cisco watching the house and the road. Nobody will get by without them knowing."

Sam speaks again, "Okay, I'm going to give Betty a call to make sure everything is going fine up there. You keep watching for McDermott and let me know the minute he shows up again. We should find him and get him out of the mix altogether. While you are waiting for that, I'll go over to David and Coleen's place and check their situation out."

"Okay, Sam, don't worry, we'll find McDermott." He turns and leaves.

Sam tells Sherry he is going over to check on David and Coleen; he turns and heads out the door after Lone Wolf. Thirty minutes later, he is sitting in his car outside of Abraham's house. When he first arrived, he didn't see Maxx out front. He checks around the house, and he finds Maxx out cold on the ground around the back of the house. He knocks on the back door, and Coleen answers, crying.

"Coleen, what's wrong? Where is David?"

Coleen wiping her eyes says, "Some man came and said you sent him, and you wanted him to take him to Betty and her daughter. David refused, and the man hit and threaten to kill me if he didn't do it. Their heading for the plane right this minute."

"How long ago did they leave?"

"About 5 minutes, if you hurry, you can catch them before they take off." She replied.

Sam is giving her his business card says, "Okay, call my office and tell my secretary what happened and tell her to get a hold of Lone Wolf andhave him meet me at Van Nuys Airport, Hanger 121. When you finish that, could you please check on Maxx out back?"

"Okay, please, Sam, hurry." Coleen turned and headed for the phonewhile Sam headed for his car.

At Sam's office, later, we see Sherry on the phone trying to get a hold of Lone Wolf. While she is dialing, Lone Wolf walks in the front door. Sherry hangs up and runs over to Lone Wolf, "Lone Wolf, you, have to get over to

Van Nuys Airport right away Sam needs you, Hanger 121. He is going to try and stop Dave from taking off."

As Sam approaches, Van Nuys Airport, he can see Hanger 121, and he also sees David and McDermott getting out of the parked car and head toward the hanger. Sam drives around the back and parks. He goes in the back door and hides behind a crate. He is hoping that McDermott will givehim an opening, so he can get David away from him long enough to take him down. When McDermott and David walk by the crate, Sam sees his chance and jumps out at McDermott, knocking him down, at the same time he yells, "David get out of here run!" By this time McDermott is slowly recovering from the tackle, Sam laid on him, and got up and looks at Sam and speaks, "So you must be the PI Sam Ryan, I've heard so much about you from Rampulla. I don't know if I should swing at you or run."

While he is talking, he pulls out a knife from his pocket; it is a big switchblade. Itlooks nasty. Sam backs up as McDermott walks toward him. McDermott takes aswipe at Sam with the blade. Sam blocks it and throws a right cross catching him on the chin. McDermott falls back against a closed 55-gal empty storage tank it falls over. As he is falling, Sam is all over him like bees to honey.   Before McDermott has a chance to recover, Sam picks him up and hits him again. This time, it's left to the stomach, and McDermott doubles over grabbing his stomach, and Sam throws a right uppercut to thechin. He falls to the ground. As he is getting up, McDermott grabs a boardlying nearby and swings it at Sam, catching him on the side of the head.

Sam goes down hard. This time McDermott is standing over Sam and getting ready to hit him again, but Sam is too quick, and he kicks McDermott in the face with his foot. This time it is McDermott who goesdown for the count. Sam gets up and looks down at McDermott. He is lying there still. Sam knows McDermott is out, and Sam quickly stoops down and puts the cuffs on him as he turns him over onto his stomach andcloses the cuffs on his wrist. Sam stands there for a minute, and he hears footsteps behind him. He turns and sees David coming in the hanger; he has two airport security guards with him.

David speaks first, "Sam, are you okay?"

"Yeah, I'm okay." Sam turns to McDermott and says, "Okay, Mr. McDermott, where is your partner, Rampulla hiding?"

McDermott looks at him with a bloody mouth and says, "You'll find out soon enough, and you won't have long to wait."

Sam turns to the guards and speaks, "Thanks for coming guys can you put him in the back seat of my car? He points to the back door and continues, "It's parked out back, thanks. The two security guards take McDermott by the arm, push him toward the back door to where Sam's caris parked and put him in the back seat.

Lone Wolf comes running in and speaks, "Sam, are you, all right? Is everything okay?"

"Yea, sure, I have a handle on everything. Have you located Rampulla yet?"

Lone Wolf replies, "Not yet, but we will. I got your message from Sherry to get over here, and I rushed over. I have my friends looking everywhere; it is only a matter of time before we catch him."

Sam speaks, "Good, it looks as though you have everything under control. Why don't you go back to the office and I'll be back in about twohours? I'm taking our friend up to Newhall and turn him to the police so that they can book him for accessory after the fact in the murder of Betty's brother."

Lone Wolf replies, "Do you need me to go with you?"

"No, I got this one." Sam turns and heads out toward the car.

Lone Wolf leaves through the front of the hanger, and Sam goes outthe back and gets into his car.

On the ride, up to Newhall, McDermott awakes in the back seat, feeling like he was hit with a brick and spoke slowly, "Where are you taking me?"

Sam looks at McDermott through the rearview mirror and speaks, "You have a date with the judge in Newhall for the murder of Betty's brother." Sam spoke with a smile on his face and continued. "I know you didn't kill the brother, but you're involved in all this in some way. You're going away for a long time."

"You can't make that stick. You have no evidence to hold me. The Police will have to let me go." Sam doesn't answer, so McDermott continues, "I've got a lot of money," McDermott says and continues, "I'll give you half to look the other way."

Sam smiles, "It isn't enough for <u>me</u> to look the other way; you've ruined two people's lives, and the only way you're going to pay for that is a lot of time in prison. Now be quiet while I enjoy this ride."

Sam heads to Newhall. The back seat is quiet for a while. Sam looks at the rearview mirror to check on McDermott. That's when it happens. McDermott hits Sam on the head, and the lights go out. Thank God when Sam got hit on the head his whole body went limp, and his body leaned over the front seat toward the passenger's side of the car, causing his foot to slide off the gas pedal, and the vehicle comes to a stop on the side of the road. McDermott got out of the car and ran down the exit ramp.

After a while, Sam came around and was holding the right side of his head. After a minute or so, he was wide awake and turned around quickly to look into the back seat. Sam saw McDermott had gone. He checked outside the car.   He finds one set of prints leading down the exit ramp.

McDermott had too much of a head start. Sam knew that trying to pick up McDermott's trail now would be fruitless. Now he was glad he got that Carphone at Lone Wolf's request. He took the phone out from under the front seat of his car and called Lone Wolf and told him where he was.

After hanging up, he looked at the phone and thought to himself, 'One day, these phones will be small enough to put in your pocket.' Now all he had todo was wait for Lone Wolf.

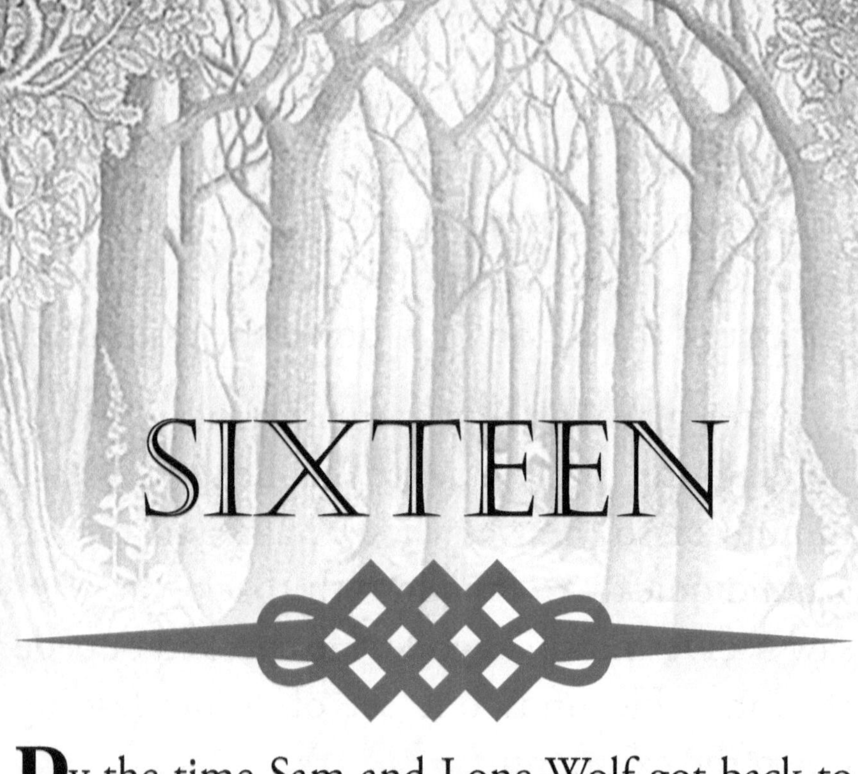

SIXTEEN

By the time Sam and Lone Wolf got back to the office, it was late afternoon. Kathy was also there. She wasn't happy she was damn right upset.

She spoke first, "Sam, can I have a word with you in your office?"

Sam knew she was upset and replied, "Sure, honey, let's go into my office." Sam followed her into the office, turned and shut the door behind them.

Kathy spoke first with this stern look on her face. "Sam, look, I know more than anyone what you went through when I got shot, but this time it's different. I sat in that chair all morning wondering if you were lying on the side of a road lifeless or not. I was worried sick all morning." Her eyes started to water, and her face looks like she is going to cry.

Sam ran to her, put his arms around her, and spoke, "Oh, Honey, I didn't mean to worry you like this. I'm sorry, but I wasn't in any danger. He just wanted to get away, not kill me." Now trying to make light of it, he continues, "Lone Wolf and I will find him again, and that will be that."

Kathy looked up at Sam's face and said, "Sam, I don't know what I would do if I ever lost you. I mean it."

Sam smiled, "Do you think I'm going to be that easy to get rid of Kathy? Now come on, give me a big smile."

Kathy smiling says, "Sam, I will always worry about you when you're on a case, and it's because I love you so much, but I don't know how many times I can go through this."

Sam puts both of his hands on each side of her face and speaks, "I want this to work between you and me, but you have to help. You know thetype of work I do is dangerous at times, and you are to have to try and deal with it in your way. I know you can. Won't you at least try for me?"

Kathy wipes her eyes and puts a friendly smile on and says, "Oh yesSam, I will, I promise I will. Now let's get back outside before Lone Wolf decides to leave.

They both turn and head toward the door, Sam opens it, and theyboth walk out to Kathy's desk. Lone Wolf is sitting at the client's chair when they come out; he has a smile on his face.

"Well, are you guys ready to get back to work? We have a killer to catch."

Everybody in the room smiles and says yes at the same time, then they all laugh. Kathy is the first to speak. "You know Sam. Lately, I've been thinking about this case, and what I've been thinking is maybe we should approach it from a different angle."

Sam speaks, "What is that Kathy?"

Kathy continues, "From the beginning, we've just been thinking that this case was just a straight-up murder of the AD, but what if it was something else."

Lone Wolf has a funny look on his face and speaks, "Like what Kathy? You've lost me."

"I'm not sure yet, but I'll have to do my research before I can speak up about it. Why don't the three of us meet here in the office in the morning, and I'll tell you all about it."

Lone Wolf slaps his hands together and stands and says, "Great guys, I love a short day. I'll see you in the morning." He starts to walk out, and Sam stops him.

"Whoa there! Big fellow, you're not finished yet. You should go into Hollywood and see if you and your friend Max can get a line on Mr. Rampulla. While you're at it, call Detective Terrana and see if he can get a line on where Mr. McDermott is. Tell him where he got out of my car by the Newhall exit. See if he can pick up his trail."

Lone Wolf's look changes from a smile to a disappointed one and says, "All right, Sam, I'll check that out and see you guys here in the morning. So long, Kathy, bye Sam."

After Lone Wolf leaves, Kathy turns to Sam and says, "Look, you already had a hard day. Why don't you go lay down at the house for a couple of hours, and when I finish here, I'll come to wake you, and you can take me out to dinner."

Sam smiles and puts his arms around Kathy and says, "Honey, you always have the best ideas." He kisses her, and Kathy laughs, and Sam walks across to the house, opens the door and goes inside. The first thing he sees is the couch, and it looked good. He walked over to it and flopped down on to the soft pillows that were there.

Meanwhile, back at the office, Kathy is working away at the case. She had this idea yesterday about the slain AD Mr. Strand back in the day, and she wanted to look up some background on him. She gets lost in thought, and the time flies. She looks up at the clock on her desk, and it says five-thirty in the evening she didn't realize she had been at it for three hours. She shuts the computer off and decides to wake up Sam, so he can take her to out to eat. She was excited about what she found out and couldn't wait to tell him at dinner. She walked across the garage and usedher brand-new shiny key to open the door. It was the first time she used it.Afterward, she put it back in her purse and walked up to the couch. She loves to watch Sam sleeping; she really couldn't explain why she just did. After a minute or so, she bent down and kissed Sam on the cheek, his eyes opened slowly, and he smiled.

"What's up, honey?" He said as he swung his feet onto the floor and rubbed his eyes.

Kathy, in an excited voice, says, "I found out something you will be delighted to hear." Then she looked serious for a minute and continued, "That is if you are still taking me to dinner."

Sam is all awake now and stands up and says, "Why are we waiting? Where do you want to eat? Name it and where there."

Kathy is standing with a smile on her face and her index finger under the chin and says, "Let me see this is a special occasion, so let's go to the Chart House over in the Marina."

Sam smiling back, says, "Sounds like a plan. Let's go" He grabs her hand pulls her to the door, and they leave.

Sam pulls into the Chart House parking lot. He surprised there is a space right next to the door which he has never been able to get. Sam smiles and gets out of the car. Kathy is standing there waiting for him when he walks around the car and takes her hand. She likes that it makes her feel good when he holds her hand. They go inside and get seated. Sam was rested from a couple of hour's nap that he had while Kathy worked at the office. They ordered their usual order. When the waiter turned and walked away, Sam turned to Kathy and clapped his hands together and said, "Well, what did you find out that was so good?"

Kathy sat there smiling she didn't want to say anything until Lone Wolf was present at the meeting in the morning, but she felt like she had to give Sam a little hint. He was sitting there with that little boy grin, and she couldn't resist that, so she says, "Mr. Strand and that's all I'm going to say until the morning meeting when Lone Wolf is present too."

"Mr. Strand?" Sam replies that's it. That's all you're going to say?"

"Yep, that's all I'm going to say." Kathy then continues, "So no more questions about that. Let's talk about something else."

Sam is now determined to find out tonight, so he says, "Alright, so how did your day go? What did you do?"

Kathy starts laughing as the lady in the next booth turns to see what was going on. Then she continues to speak, "You're not going to get it out of me that easy, so you might as well forget it and change the subject."

Sam puts that pouting grin on his face and says, "Okay, okay, we'll forget about it for now. But it better be worthwhile."

"It will be I promised," Kathy replies.

After a few minutes of silence, the waiter brings the order, and they both begin to eat. Sam never took his eyes off Kathy as he ate. By the time they finished eating, that look had turned into the loving stare.

They ordered some coffee after they eat then sit there staring at eachother. Sam reaches across the table and holds Kathy's hand. Sam speaks, "You do know that I love you."

Kathy smiles and says, "Why don't we go home and go into that in more detail."

SEVENTEEN

Sam and Kathy are standing at the door to the house, and Sam takes off Kathy's jacket and speaks, "You won't need that jacket where we're going."

Kathy smiles as Sam. They both go inside and head toward the bedroom. Sam is standing by the bed; he starts to undress her. The blouse falls to the floor, and next, he pulls her skirt off, and she steps out of it.

Kathy speaks first, "You know I'm beginning to enjoy this."

"Shall I continue?"

Kathy says. "Yes"

Kathy takes off Sam's shirt and ties and unbuckles his pants. They fall to the floor. Sam steps out of them. They stand there for a moment, and Kathy kisses Sam and pushes him back onto the bed, and then she lies on top of him and kisses him. "Now you can go into detail about that phrase, 'I love you.'" The night continues, and it becomes a time of love, passion as they again become one for a while.

Morning comes quickly as they both awake next to one another. Kathy speaks first. You are considering his smiling eyes, "Good morning. Come on; we should be at the office. You want to shower first?"

Sam smiles and says, "Why don't we both go in there?"

Kathy laughs as she swings around to the edge of the bed. "Oh no, we can't do that. We'll never get to the office. You lay there while I take my shower first." She rises and puts on her bathrobe and heads to the bathroom as Sam watches that vision of beauty disappear behind the door.

Sam and Kathy cross the garage to the office and open the door and go in. Kathy heads to her desk to retrieve all the information she found out yesterday. Just then, Lone Wolf opens the front door and walks up to Kathy's desk. "Good morning Kathy and how are you this bright and sunny morning."

Kathy looks up from the desk and speaks. "Good morning Lone Wolf, I'm fine, thank you c' mon, I'm headed to Sam's office for that meeting. There is some fresh coffee over there on the desk that Sam just made."

After Lone Wolf gets some coffee, he follows Kathy into Sam'soffice, and they both sit across from Sam.

Sam speaks first, "Okay, I'm going to turn this meeting over to Kathy. She says she may have some new insight into the case." Then he looks to Kathy and continues, "Kathy, you have the floor."

Kathy stands and faces the others and starts, "I've asked you here this morning because I think we have been looking at this case all wrong.

Now, to begin, we assumed that the AD of that Movie that was murdered back in the seventies was murdered because he wouldn't help get the family a foot in the door of the movie industry, but what if he got killed because of something he did to the family in New Jersey. Now I did some backgroundchecks on Mr. Strand, and the first thing I found out was that his real name was Mr. Sean O'Conner, and Mr. O!Conner was from New Jersey, and he worked for the family as a go-between for the Cartel in Mexico and the family dealing with drugs. To start with, he had his movie studio in Hollywood on Gower Street. It was called Monarch Studio. It was a small studio that made a lot of movies in Mexico. A lot of his movies were made in Mexico, so it was easy for him to import cocaine and other drugs into the States in all his equipment. At first, he was doing it with the help of the Donnelly family back east."

Then Lone wolf jumps up to speak, "I bet I can finish this story. He decided to keep some for himself. So, he made a deal with the Cartel in Mexico to sell some of the drugs here in California and kept the profits forhimself, and the family found out and killed him."

Lone Wolf sits back down and puts a satisfying smile on his face likehe just beat the bad guys.

Kathy continues, "You are right, Lone Wolf now to continue my story, so after Mrs. Langdon had that little meeting with Mr. Strand and Mrs. Langdon was in the bathroom freshening up. Mr. Rampulla came in and killed Mr. Strand. He didn't know at the time Mrs. Langdon was in the other room. Mr. Rampulla found that out later. That's when he started hunting her down. She was a witness to the murder, but more important, Mr. Rampulla didn't know what she knew besides the obvious, so she had to go. So, Ms. Langdon thought that to be safe and keep her husband out of it, and she would be better off by going into hiding."

Sam wants to put his two cents in "Kathy, that's all well and good, but how does that help us with our problem?"

Kathy speaks, "If we can find out who told the Donnelly family back in New Jersey, then we are one step closer to finding out where Mr. Rampulla is. We might even find out who he reports to while he is out here."

"Okay, so what is our next step?" Lone Wolf asks.

Sam speaks "Lone Wolf, and I will go over to Monarch Studios and check it out while you call my friend in New Jersey. I left his number on your desk. You ask him if he knows where there is a list of people that worked at Monarch Studios when it was a working studio. M y friend was a financial advisor when the studio was at its peak, and he would know. We'll all meet back here tonight around five."

Lone Wolf speaks, "I know a friend that knows the watchman at the old studio he should be able to get Sam and me in without any trouble."

Sam speaks, "Well, let's go, Lone Wolf."

They head toward the door and leave. About twenty minutes later, they reach Gower Street and park the car and get out.

Sam speaks first, "Okay, on this slip of paper that Kathy gave me, the address is 140 Gower Street."

Lone Wolf jumps in and says, "There across the Street look the sign says Monarch Studio. At least the building is still there."

"Yea, let's see if anyone is home."

Sam and Lone Wolf cross the street and head for the front gate. Behind the gate stands an elderly gentleman in a guard uniform.

The guard is facing Lone wolf and speaks, "Gentlemen, can I help you?"

Sam speaks, "Yes, we would like to come in and have a look-see. Would that be possible?"

The guard looks at Sam and says, "That would not be possible, sir. Why do you wish to look around this studio, it's closed and has been closed a long time, since 1981? What business do you have here? Who sent you?"

Lone Wolf speaks with a smile on his face, "Well, a Mr. Albert Jones sends his regards, and he told me you would let us look around." As he is talking, he hands the guard the money through the bars.

The guard takes the money, and with a smile, he says, "Well, if Mr. Jones says you could, I guess that would be alright." He takes the money and uses a key to open the gate wide enough for them both to go in, then he continues, "What would like to see first?"

Sam speaks, "How long did this studio stay open, and when did it close?"

The guard reaches in his pocket and pulls out his pipe and proceeds to light it and says, "Well first like I said before it closed back in eighty-one that was right after Mr. Strand got himself killed. Mr. Strand was the owner, along with Mr. Chandler. After his death, Mr. Chandler let the bank take this place over. The studio wasn't making much money anyway and had Mr. Strand lived; the bank would probably have taken it anyway. The Studio only made a half a dozen movies, and they weren't hits. At least not by the industry standards. They were all Westerns, and they were made on location somewhere in Mexico. Come on, and I'll show you where the offices were."

While they walked down the street through a set that looked like the old west, Sam was thinking it would be great to be making a western on a set like this one with him as the hero, of course. He would be walking down the street heading toward the Saloon to have it out with the bad guy named Iron Mike. He was getting into it when he heard a voice. It was Lone Wolf speaking.

"Hey Sam, this set looks like an old town in the west, doesn't it? Makes you want to put a pair of guns on and mosey down the street." Lone Wolf laughs.

Sam speaks, "Yea, Lone Wolf, just be careful you don't get shot."

Then the guard spoke, "Those offices are over there behind the Saloon. We should turn down that street. He points over by the saloon, andthey head down that street. Just then, a shot rang out and landed right near Lone Wolf. Lone Wolf took cover behind the water trough, and Sam dove into an open doorway of what was supposed to be the barbershop. Sam was now looking out the doorway and in the direction of the gunshot. Sam was thinking now why someone would be shooting at us? What the hell is going on? Sam had his gun out and was looking to see where the direction was that the shot came. Sam sees a shadow down the street behind the stairs. Then the figure disappeared behind the building. Sam took out after him, but by the time he got to the stairs, the person was gone. Sam put his gun away and told Lone Wolf he could come out now the shooting was over. Lone Wolf stands cautiously while looking at Sam.

He starts to speak. "Jesus Sam, what the hell is going on around here? Someone could get killed."

Sam speaks, "I don't know, but something tells me somebody doesn't want us snooping around here."

While all this commotion was going on, the watchman disappeared. Sam and Lone Wolf head toward the main gate.

Sam speaks first, "Well, it looks like just another day in paradise."

Lone Wolf replies, "Sam if I'm going to get shot at, I need a gun. Let us go now. I don't think we're wanted."

Sam speaks, "I think you're right, but we're not leaving yet. I want tospeak to the watchman again. Let's head over toward the front gate. I'm sure he's over there."

Sam and Lone Wolf arrive at the front gate just as a police car pullsup, and two policemen get out. The first policeman is tall, about six feet two or three. He had a smile on his face when he spoke. "Okay, who was the gentleman that put acall in about a shooting on the studio lot?"

The guard came out of his shack and started talking nervously "I did I was showing them the old west set, and we were on our way to the offices when someone fired at us. Just one shot, but it scared the hell out of me, and I ran straight back here and called you guys."

The policeman turned and looked at Sam and spoke, "What were you guys doing on the set?"

Sam takes out his credentials and shows them to the officer, "Myname is Sam Ryan, and I was here because one of my clients, she had a connection with one of the owners of this studio, and I was looking for some information."

"Did any of you see who shot at you?"

Lone Wolf speaks, "No, sir, but his shot came pretty close to me. I didn't have a gun to shoot back, so I just jumped behind the water trough."

The officer spoke, "Give my partner your name and where we can get in touch with you, then you can go and don't leave town." Then looking at the guard, he continued, "C' mon I want you to take me to where you thought the shot came from. Now I want to look around." Sam stood there, watching the guard and the policeman as they headed off in the direction of the western set.

Sam turned to see Lone Wolf talking to the other policeman, "C' mon I want to get back to the office. Did you give the officer the info he wanted?"

Lone Wolf replied, "Yep, that should do it. Let's go."

Lone Wolf and Sam turn and head toward the car. When they got back to the office, it was mid-afternoon, and in Southern California, at that time of the day, it means a six-letter phrase that no one likes to say, 'It's Hot.' They were glad to get inside where the air conditioner was on, and it was nice and cool. Sam speaks first, "Kathy, see if you can find who oversaw the Mexican Division of Monarch Studio when they were open for business. Oh, yea did my friend from New Jersey call back yet?"

Kathy replies, "No, he hasn't, but give me a few minutes, and I'llhave that other information for you."

Sam turns back to Lone Wolf and speaks, "Now Lone Wolf, we needto find out who was upset when the Studio went under and who would stand to lose the most."

Lone Wolf smiles and says, "Well, we know why Mr. Strand is dead. He wouldn't help the family get a foot in the door out here, and we know that Ms. Langdon was in hiding because she saw Mr. Strand shot. The onlyother people I can think of that would lose something if the studio closed would be the Cartel's, and that's only if and this is a big if the studio was acting as a mule for the Cartel."

Sam jumped up off the couch and pointed to Lone Wolf with a smileand said, "Now you're starting to think like a P.I." He turned to Kathy at the computer and said, "Kathy, see if you can find any Mexicans in key positions at the studios that might be connected."

Kathy smiled and said, "I'm on it." She starts to type away on thekeyboard with a smile.

Sam could see she was enjoying this part of the case. She loved to research and loved to find people on the computer database. In the meantime, Sam turns to Lone Wolf and says, "Now, why would anybody be shooting at us this morning at the studio?" Then pointing at Lone Wolf, he continues, "Unless they thought we were getting to close to finding something they didn't want us to find." Then as though a light bulb came onover his head, Sam snaps his finger and says, "Lone Wolf, we are going back to Monarch Studios tonight. Only this time we will be ready for anything. In the meantime, let's wait and see how many names Kathy finds on her employee list for Monarch Studio."

Lone Wolf has a look of concern and speaks, "You know Sam, I would feel a lot better if I could carry a gun. This job is getting dangerous."

"Lone Wolf, you know we put in an application a few weeks ago. You know how slow the wheels turn in this city. Don't worry, and you'llget it any day now."

Lone Wolf smiles and says, "Yea, but I would like to have it before I'm shot dead."

Just then, Kathy looks up and says to Sam, "I got it, Sam. There was only one listing for that position, and that name is Hector Gomez he had an apartment right here in the Valley. It's not far from here." She writes down the address and gives it to Sam.

Sam takes it, reads it, and says, "It's on Cartwright that's just down the street from the Post Office. Come on Lone Wolf let us take a little ride over there and see what we can find out. Afterward, we can head back to Monarch Studio.

Lone Wolf has a worried look on his face and speaks, "Can't we waituntil the mail arrives maybe my gun permit will be in it."

Kathy laughs out loud and speaks to Lone Wolf, "Oh, Lone Wolf, it will be okay. You're not afraid of the other big bad Wolves, are you?" She laughs some more.

Lone Wolf tugs on his leather vest at the bottom and sticks out his chest and says, "No, of course, you don't know me when I get angry. I scare myself sometimes he turns and follows Sam out the door." We hear Sam telling Lone Wolf they would stop back here before they go to the Studio and see if the permit came in the mail.

A few minutes later, as they were heading toward Cartwright-street, Lone Wolf looks at Sam and says, "You know Sam sometimes I wonder if Kathy likes me or not."

Sam looks back at Lone Wolf and says, "Oh, she likes you fine shelikes to ride you sometimes to keep you on your toes. I wouldn't worry about it. Now tell me, what is the number of that house on Cartwright?"

Lone Wolf looks down at the paper Kathy gave him with the address on it and said, "Let's see its 6306 Cartwright Ave, right?"

"Okay, that should be right up here on the left. Yep there it is right here" as Sam points to the house and continues, "Nice looking place, I'll just pull into the driveway." Sam stops the car, and they both get out and walk to the front door. Sam knocks, and they both wait for an answer.

After a few minutes, a middle-aged man comes to the door and talks through the screen door looks at Sam and says, "Yeah, can I help you, Senor?"

Sam looks at him cautiously speaks, "I'm sorry to bother you, but we're looking for Hector Gomez. Can you tell me if he is home?"

The man behind the screen door speaks, "Who wants to know?"

Sam replies, "I'm sorry I'm a Private Investigator, and we are looking to talk to him."

It was about that time the man bolted to the rear of the house, Sam looks at Lone Wolf and says backdoor. At the same time, Lone Wolf heads for the back of the house. Sam opens the screen door and chases him to theback door. By the time the man reaches the end of the house and opens theback door, Lone Wolf is waiting for him and catches him with his right fistright on the jaw. The man goes down as Sam comes through the door.

"Good work Lone Wolf help him up, and we'll have a little chat withhim."

Then the surprised man is helped up by Lone Wolf and starts speaking, "I didn't do it, I didn't do it."

Sam laughs and says, "Then why did you run, and what didn't you do?"

The man looks at Sam then moves his jaw, I guess he was checking to see if Lone Wolf had broken it. Then he says, "Why did you hit me?"

Lone Wolf smiles and says, "I was just making sure you wouldn't go anywhere."

Sam looks at the man with a stern look and says, "Now are you, Hector Gomez?"

The smiles back weakly and says, "Yea, what do you want with me?"

Sam answers, "We only wanted to ask you how long you had worked for Monarch Studio when it was up and running well?"

"Why didn't you say so, you didn't have to hit me to get an answer. Let me see," the man continues, "I was there when… It opened for business in 1955, and I was there until it closed in 1981, so that would be twenty-six years. Yep, that's right." The man continued, "I used to find the right locations in Mexico for the filming. I would go there first, and they would follow afterward with a crew."

"Did you know a Mister Strand he was an Assistant Director for the studio?"

"Mr. Strand let me see" He continues to think about it for a minute then continues, "Yea, now I remember he was loaned out to another studio to do a picture with Marilyn Monroe, Tony Curtis, and Jack Lemon. After that, he was shot under very mysterious circumstances. I don't think they ever found the man that did it. Mister Crew was my boss back then. I would report to him."

"Can you tell me where Mr. Crew is today?"

"Oh, he was killed in Mexico back in 1982. It was a car accident. They never did find the body. The car and Mr. Crews went over a cliff and into the river. They found the car, but the body well they figured it went downstream. They never did recover it."

"Did Mr. Crews have any family?"

"Yes, as a matter of fact, Mrs. Crew lives in Reseda. I'm not sure of the address. I haven't seen her since she lost her husband, I went to the funeral, you know, but I believe she still lives in the same place."

Sam speaks, "Well, I guess that will be all for now. Stay around. We might have some more questions for you later. Next time don't run until you hear the question." Then he turns to

Lone Wolf and says, "C' mon we're going back to the office." Lone Wolf follows as they climb back in the car and drive off.

When Sam and Lone Wolf enter the office about twenty minutes later, Kathy is waiting for them with a smile on her face and waving a letterin the air. She starts talking. She is excited now. "Lone Wolf guess what I have in my hand?"

Lone Wolf sees the letter Kathy is holding and runs to her, trying to get the message. She keeps waving it around so Lone Wolf couldn't get it and laughing.

Lone Wolf speaks, "Kathy if you don't give me that letter, I'm goingto get Sam's permission to grab you and paddle you well."

Sam is laughing by this time and says, "Oh I don't know Lone Wolf I can't do that if I did, I would end up sleeping on the couch and I don't think I would like that."

Lone Wolf speaks, "If it is addressed to me, let me have it, Kathy."

Kathy replies, "well, it's addressed to the agency, but it's about you."

Now Lone Wolf is getting upset. So, Sam decides enough is enough and speaks, "Kathy, either let him see the letter or tell him what it says."

Kathy pulls the letter down and says, "Oh okay, it's a letter from the police department it says that your permit to carry a gun is approved, and you are supposed to bring your gun to the North Hollywood police station and sign your permit and get a picture taken."

Lone Wolf puts a big smile on his face and says, "I'm going down right now."

Just puts his hand out toward Long Wolf and says, "Lone Wolf, take the shells out unless you want to get arrested before you show them the letter."

Lone Wolf stops and turns then says, "Yea, that's right. I better, thanks." Then Lone Wolf turns and leaves.

Sam and Kathy stand there looking at one another, and Sam smiles and says, "Ah, I think I'm going to have to watch that boy."

Kathy smiles and half laughing says, "We got some work to do."

Sam agrees to say, "Yes speaking of work; I have an idea I want to run by you."

"Okay, I'm listening, Sam."

"Okay, now try to follow me on this; when we first started this case, it came to our attention that Mr. Rampulla killed Mr. Strand because Strand was stopping him from getting a foothold into one of the Major Studios at the time."

"Yea, so what's your point?" Kathy says with a curious look on her face.

Sam continues, "Well, what if Rampulla had another reason. What if he already had a foothold and Rampulla was afraid that Mr. Strand would expose it."

"Okay, now you lost me. What do you mean?"

"Well, today, when we were at the studio, and we got shot at, and itgot me thinking. What if Strand found out that they were smuggling drugs by way of the studio from Mexico, and that's why he died."

Kathy starts walking around the room taking in what Sam had just said, finally she speaks, "Do you think the shooter today had the feeling thatmaybe you were looking around the studio for drugs?"

Sam speaks with a questionable look on his face, "You think it's too farfetched?"

Kathy points the finger at Sam and says, "No, no, why else would somebody be shooting at you. They only thing is you're going to play hell trying to prove that."

"Not if we could find the drugs. The first thing we should do is go back and talk to Mr. Gomez.

EIGHTEEN

An hour had passed when Lone Wolf walked into the office excited with a smile on his face and waving something in his right hand. "I got it; I got it. I finally got it my gun permit."

Sam and Kathy stood and clapped their hands and in unison, said, "Yea, Finally!"

Lone Wolf suddenly changes from happy to humble and said, "Yeah, well, it's thanks to both of you getting me to apply and going to the class. Thanks, guys."

Then Sam says in passing, "Yeah, well, don't go and shoot someoneor you by accident, Kathy and I will have to write up the paperwork. Okay, now that that's over I got to talk to you about something concerning the case. I've already explained it to Kathy."

Lone Wolf smiles and says, "Okay, Boss, what's that?"

"Well, I'll explain it on the way over to see Mr. Hector Gomez."

Lone Wolf speaks with a puzzled look on his face and says, "Hector Gomez? But we just saw him earlier, and he didn't have anything to say."

"That's because we didn't ask him the right questions. C'mon, I'll explain it in the car on the way."

"I was telling Kathy, what if Mister Strand wasn't killed by Mister Rampulla for trying to stop him from trying to get the Mob a foot in the door. What if he is dead because he found out something more sinister?"

Lone Wolf speaks, "You lost me their boss. I mean, what could be more sinister then killing someone?"

"Maybe sinister is the wrong word." Sam thinks for a minute and says, "Intriguing. That's it what if Mister Strand is dead because he found out that the studio was transporting drugs from Mexico into the country using props and equipment?"

Lone Wolf now has a look of disbelief, "Are you serious, what gave you that idea?"

Sam comes back with, "Think about it why would someone take a shot at us today when we were looking in the studio? I   mean,   can you think of a better reason for them to take a shot?"

"Okay say you're right, how do we prove it?"

Sam looks over at Lone Wolf and says, "Well first we go to Hector Gomez and see if he knows anything about that. That's a start. Right now, it's the only lead we have, so I say let's do it."

Lone Wolf has an excited look on his face and says, "I say, let's do it right now."

A half-hour later, Sam Ryan and Lone Wolf are sitting in the car right outside Hector Gomez's house. Sam speaks to Lone Wolf "Okay now listen, we give him the soft approach."

Lone Wolf smiles and says, "Yea, and if that doesn't work?"

Sam shrugs his shoulders and says, "Well then, I'll let you talk to him." Lone Wolf smiles as they both climb out of the car and head toward Hector's house. When they get to the door, they knock. It was a few minutes before Hector came to the door, opened it, and smiled said, "Heynice to see you again. Come on in."

Sam and Lone Wolf walked into the living room and sat on the sofa. Hector walked in behind them and sat on the chair. He looked at the two of them and said, "I didn't expect to see you two guys so soon. How can I help?"

Sam and Lone Wolf look at each other, and then Sam looks at Hector and says, "The last time we spoke to you, you told us you would find locations down in Mexico for them to film."

Hector replies, "Yes, that's right, so?"

Sam continues, "Well, can you tell us exactly where in Mexico theydid the filming?"

Hector speaks, "Yea sure it was about fifteen miles southeast of Tijuana. In a little town called Miquel."

Sam looks at Lone Wolf like he was going to ask the question of the year, (well I guess it was in a way) anyway he looks back at Hector and says, "Did they ever bring back anything that wasn't normal from Miquel to the states that you know of?"

You could see the look in Hector's eyes that he remembered something, but he wasn't sure he should say anything about it. So, Sam spoke again. "C' mon Hector you need to tell us. We're going to find out sooner or later, and if you tell us now, it will go easier on you later."

Hector replied, "Well, I'm sure it is anything at all, I remember one time that I went, and I did go all the time. We were on the way back from Miquel Mexico, and the trucks with all the equipment stopped in Downey at the

Warehouse. We were only there for about an hour. Then we headed on into the Los Angeles Warehouse to unload the equipment and trucks."

Sam looks at Lone Wolf and says, "Well, you know our next step?"

Lone Wolf replies, "Yes, we have to go to the Downey Warehouse, and we have to find those drugs and turn them over to the police." Lone Wolf looks at Sam and says, "Er Sam, how are we going to that?"

"Let's get back to the office and figure it out." Sam and Lone Wolfhead out the door and head back to the office. When they get back to the office, Kathy and Sherry are waiting.

Lone Wolf speaks first, "We don't know who or what is at the Warehousewaiting for us remember Sam, we are the only ones that have gun permits. My guys don't have anything."

Sam has the look of a man whose light bulb over his head went on, "Lone Wolf, how many of your guys can you get that all have bikes?"

Suddenly a big smile comes on Lone Wolf's face, and he says, "I getit, we outnumber them and fight them with sticks and pipes if we have to."

"Right, how bikers with their bikes can you get in an hour?"

Lone Wolf jumps up and says "maybe thirty or so. The <u>sound</u> alonecould scare the daylights out of them."

"Well, at least confuse the hell out of them. Okay, you make calls and do whatever you should get them there, by seven-pm tonight. Give them the address and tell them to be at the warehouse by seven-pm. We will get there, you and me by six-thirty tonight, that will give us enough time to set up the scenario. Now go makes the calls. I should make somecalls myself. I'll meet you back here at five-pm tonight, got it?"

"I'm gone; meet you back here at five sharp." Lone Wolf leaves, and Sam heads for the office to make some calls.

Just before he picks up the phone, it rings, and he picks it up and says, "Hello, Sam Ryan detective agency, Sam Ryan speaking." There is a pause, and then Sam speaks, "Oh hello, Detective Terrana, what can I do for you?" There is a minute of silence, and then Sam speaks, "Detective Terrana, can you hold him until I call you back?

Another silence and then, "Great, yes, you can hold him for at least forty-eight hours. Great thanks for the help." Sam hangs up and goes outside to tell everyone the good news. Sherry is sitting at her desk, and Kathy is standing next to her, they are both looking at Sam. Sam speaks, "That was from Detective Terrana he has Mr. McDermott in custody, and he is going to hold him for forty-eight hours."

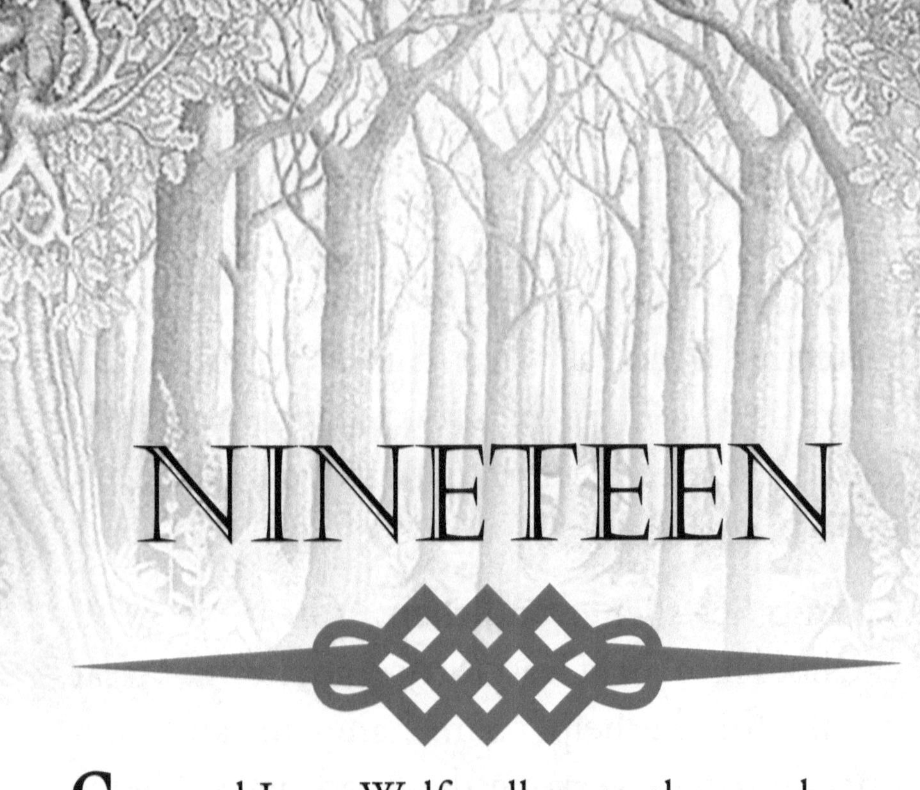

NINETEEN

Sam and Lone Wolf pull up to the warehouse in Downey. Sam checks his watch and looks at Lone Wolf and says, "All right, it is now five-twenty-seven. Let's check around back first." They both get out of the car and head around back.

When they get there, they see the office to the warehouse, and the lights are on. Sam quietly says, "We'll check the office first now be quiet."

They move closer to the building, and that is about the time Lone Wolf accidentally kicks a can lying on the ground. It makes a noise as it hits the building, and they both run for cover. One of the men from the office opens the door and looks out. He doesn't see Sam hiding behind the fifty-five-gallon drums, and Lone Wolf made to some canvas covering. The man goes back to the office and closes the door. Sam looks at Lone Wolf mad but doesn't say anything. They move to the window of the office and look in.

Sam looks at Lone Wolf and says quietly, "You cover me, I'm going in." Lone Wolf gives him the acknowledged nod of the head.

Sam stoops low and walks to the door, once in front he banks open the door and says, "Hello boys, going somewhere?"

Mr. Rampulla is sitting at the desk with three goons near him. Mr. Rampulla speaks first. "Well, if it isn't the Hollywood P.I. Out for a stroll, are you?"

Sam speaks, "Don't move any of you. Just take out your guns and lay them on the floor. We got you covered from outside."

All of a sudden, you could hear a lot of rumbling getting closer and louder by the minute. "You hear that noise? That's the Calvary coming to Mr. Rampulla; you're finished."

Mr. Rampulla starts to look around to find a way out, so did the rest of his men, but they couldn't they knew them too late. Lone Wolf walks in with a gun in hand and says, "Well looks like we have some bad guys in trouble here. You heard him drop those guns." The bad guys all look at eachother and start putting their guns on the ground, all but one. Mr. Rampulla pulls his gun out and stands to try to shoot Sam, but Sam already has his gun pulled and shoots Mr. Rampulla right between the eyes, and he falls back onto the seat dead. The bikes are still making a lot of noise and coming in and out of the warehouse.

Sam looks at Lone Wolf and says, "We'll ask those guys outside to turn off their bikes and check the warehouse to see if we have the drugs we are looking for, and I'll call the police."

Lone Wolf turns and leaves as Sam turns to the bad guy and says, "All right if you guys don't want the same thing he got (pointing to Mr. Rampulla) move over there and sit in those seats and be quiet while I make the call." The men moved over to settle in the seats. Sam walks over to the desk, the whole holding the gun at the men and picks up the phone with the empty hand and dials the police. Meantime Lone Wolf comes in and tells Sam, "We found the drugs; there is more than we thought."

Sam looks at Lone Wolf and says, "Good now, all we have to do now is wait for the police to come."

EPILOGUE

The next day Sam called Kathy and asked her to come to the office and then called Lone Wolf and asked him to also come to the office. When everybody arrived, Sam tried to explain what happened last night.

Sam spoke, "About an hour after the police took Mr. Rampulla's body and the bad guys into custody. They had to have another truck to get the drugs. I got a call from Detective Terrana in Newhall. He told me he found Mr. Rampulla's fingerprints all over Ms. Langdon's brother's apartment, which cinched Mr. Rampulla for the murder of her brother. Oh, and Lone Wolf I saved the best for last. The Downey Police Department is going to give all the bikers that were present at the warehouse a commendation, and that includes you, Lone Wolf. The Captain said, and I'm quoting him now. He said they confused the bad guys with all the noiselong enough for us to get the drop on them."

Kathy and Lone Wolf started laughing, then Lone Wolf spoke, "That's funny Sam, but you deserve a lot of the credit, and after all, it was your idea, so congratulations on your first case in California. So, what happens to Ms. Langdon and her daughter now?"

Sam speaks, "Actually, it's my second case. Well anyway, Ms. Langdon will collect that two-million-dollar life insurance policy from her husband, and she and her daughter will live happily ever after wherever they go. As for Mr. McDermott, they are going to send him back to New Jersey. It seems the police there want to talk to him about some past crimes."

Everybody laughed, and then Kathy spoke next, "Well, I'm glad it's all over. Just between you and me, I want you to know that knowing you can be dangerous to my health. I think I'll stick to being your secretary and let what happens, happen."

Lone Wolf says, "Well, these family squabbles are over my head, soI'm going to the bar, you know my bar in Hollywood and reunite with my family."

Sam Looks at Kathy and says with a smile, "Oh, I'm having a partyfor Lone Wolf's 'family' at Maxx's Place, Now End of story."

They both laughed.